High Explorations

Sexy Stories Collection

VOLUME 32

6 EROTIC SHORT STORIES

GACY HARPER

Publisher's Note: This is a work of fiction. Names,
characters, places, and incidents are a product of
the author's imagination. Locales and public
names are sometimes used for atmospheric
purposes. Any resemblance to actual people, living
or dead, or to businesses, companies, events,
institutions, or locales is completely coincidental.

High Explorations/ Gacy Harper. -- 1st ed.
Xplicit Press, an imprint of TLM Media LLC

ISBN-13: 978-1-62327-563-1
ISBN-10: 1-62327-563-6
eISBN: 978-1-62327-614-0

Printed in the United States of America

CONTENTS

1 ENCRYPTION

Fuckers Anon had pretty much eaten away an entire week of his pay. And though he didn't give a rat's ass about that, he was sure the landlord would. So, he had to come up with the rent money—and fast. If not, he'd be out on the street in a week's time, and he didn't think he'd like living in some fucking box, with nowhere to plug in his laptop.

Letting out a sigh, he sat at his desk and booted up his PC. "Fucking rent-mongers," he thought disgustingly as he typed in his password, sucking him dry like some two-bit whore, and all he had to show for it was a cheap-ass roach motel they called an apartment. Well, he'd show them. He'd get them their fucking money, and they could leave him the fuck alone. He had a week and that was more than enough time. But his hand trembled with doubt as he clicked on the Nympho Warriors game icon on his desktop.

He needed to relax. And playing the game relaxed him as nothing else did. He told himself he wasn't addicted, but he knew he was. "Fuck it," he mumbled, running a hand thru his dark hair. A man was entitled to relax, so he was gonna relax. Sitting back in his chair, he put the virtual goggles on, and let the world of nymphos fill his head.

Rich, dark, vibrant colors swirled, twisted inside his brain, and he felt the heady rush of pleasure pain as he was ripped body and soul from his chair and transported into a fantasy world of lust and power known as the realm of Myludium. When his feet landed on cobbled stones, he took a deep breath and, reaching into the satchel at his waist, pulled out the sacred stone of desire.

The effervesce sky around him glowed red and green. Trees swayed as a blue mist came over the horizon, moving towards him. He held the sacred stone high, and as the mist drew closer, the stone began to heat in his hands. Three Nympho Warriors walked out of the mist; one with skin the color of deep dark chocolate, the kind that melted in your mouth. Another had milky white skin and flaming red hair, while the third had skin that was tanned and lean, with mysterious amber eyes. All three were naked, wearing only the gold bands of their tribe around their neck. When the mist cleared, their leader—the one with skin like rich coco butter and breasts large enough to fill a man's hand—stepped forward and stood before him expectantly. He bowed deeply, offering her the stone.

"Mistress Kyra, may I present you with this humble gift."

"Welcome back, Lord Darius. We've been waiting for your return." Smiling seductively, she took the stone, squeezed it, and it became a pale yellow foam that oozed between her fingers.

She rubbed the yellow foam over her dark skin as the other two women stepped forward and began to undress him. "Ah, Lady Ivy," he said to the woman with flaming red hair. "A pleasure to see you again. And Mirabelle."

They took their time undressing him. Slow, oh, so painfully slow, teasing him with their feathery touches. His cock was rock hard and more than ready for his welcome back party. He met Kyra's liquid brown eyes and watched as she began to glow and sparkle, preparing her for the ceremony that was about to begin. In her eyes, he saw that she was ready too.

He stood there naked, his seven-inch cock standing proud and tall when a stone slab appeared out of the shadows. They led him over to it, and Kyra proceeded to lie down on the slab, opening her legs for him, inviting him to taste the dewy nectar between her dark, golden thighs.

Quickly, he went to work, taking her clit into his mouth and teasing the tiny morsel with his tongue. He sucked, nibbled, and inhaled the ripe scent of her, all the while digging his fingers into her ass and kneading the tender flesh. She vibrated beneath his hands and his mouth, while his tongue dipped in and out of her, his teeth biting, tugging at her clit. She balled her hands into his hair and urged his head forward, and on a sigh of pleasure, demanded he take more.

He eagerly took what she offered while the other two moved over him, around him, rubbing against his back, his sides. Lady Mirabelle nipped and licked his back, from his neck down to his ass, drawing tiny, wet circles on his hot skin with her mouth. She ran her tongue along the edges of his butt crack, turning like smooth silk between his legs to lick his balls. And while she licked, nibbled, and sucked urgently on his balls, Lady Ivy knelt at his feet and took his swollen cock into her mouth. Together, they began a dance older than time all the while dragging him deeper and deeper into a pool of molten pleasure.

While the two sat at his feet and drove him crazy, using their hands and mouths on him, he kept darting his tongue in and out of Kyra's dark pussy, drawing her sweet honeydew into his mouth. He plundered, gorged, and feasted, and when she started to moan and move more aggressively against him, he spread her butt cheeks and jammed two fingers into her ass.

Kyra let out a loud sigh of pleasure, arching her hips forward as she dared him to do more, to give her more. He continued to move his fingers in and out of her ass while his mouth and tongue lapped and tugged on the lips of her womanhood. His cock stretched and strained, as Ivy and Mirabelle took turns deep throating him, driving him hard and fast.

On a groan, he reared up, took both of Kyra's dark, golden tits in his hands, and began to suckle. He bit roughly on one taunt nipple, pulling it hard with his teeth, wrapping his tongue around the chocolate orb. Squeezing her tits tightly, he tasted the salty scent of her, and the heady aroma pulled at him, forming a tight fist in his gut. He ran his mouth along the deep curvature of her breasts, up to the hollow of her shoulder, leaving a heated, wet trail in its wake. Taking her ear lobe between his teeth, he bit gently, his breath heavy and hot. Beneath his hands, she quivered like a fine-tune bow, and giving her tits one last squeeze, he slid on top of her and rammed himself hard inside her wet pussy as his mouth caught her cry of pleasure with a searing kiss.

Their tongues mingled, melded, as they moved together in perfect rhythm. She matched him beat for beat, stride for stride, their bodies flowing as one. Lady Ivy slid up along his right side, Lady Mirabelle his left, their hands and mouths moving up his fevered skin, while their long, silky-smooth legs wrapped around his. While he pounded his cock into Kyra's hot wet pussy, they bit, they nibbled, their long nails clawing at him.

Faster and harder—all the while, the ball of need grew larger, consuming him. Lady Ivy grabbed him by the hair and turned his head to her, capturing his mouth with hers. She assaulted his mouth, running her tongue along his cheek, his teeth and gums, before capturing his tongue with her teeth. He found it difficult to breath, and his only thought was "oh yeah" when Lady Mirabelle climbed on his back and began to grind her wet, hot cunt into his lower back.

The three of them rocked and rolled in

sync, their bodies sliding, glistening in the cool Myludium night. Lady Mirabelle slid off his back, and pulling out of Kyra's pussy, he shot his hot cum onto her belly as the orgasm exploded inside him.

Both Ivy and Mirabelle dipped their fingers into his cum and bringing it to their lips, licked their fingers clean. He stood there watching them, as they bent over Kyra and proceeded to lap up his seed. In the distance, he heard the sound of thunder rolling as he balled a hand in their hair and pulled their heads close. He needed to taste them, to taste his cum on them. Thunder boomed when he took the ruby red lips of Lady Ivy, and as he inhaled the musty scent of him on her tongue, the night sky crackled as silver stars danced above his head.

Kyra rose from the stone slab, her beautiful big tits in her hands, and rubbed them against his arm. Turning his head, he captured the mouth of Lady Mirabelle, the taste of him warm and inviting on her breath. Not to be outdone, Kyra moved behind him, trailing kisses along his shoulder, his back. She massaged his shoulders and rubbed her wet cunt against his ass. Around him, above him, thunder ripped the sky, echoing in his head.

Lady Ivy and Mirabelle pulled slowly away from him, leaving behind soft, wet kisses. With his arms extended, palms up, each placed in his hands a sacred stone of desire. Looking at them, he smiled and then watched as each one floated back into the blue mist that had begun to form around him.

Behind him, Kyra cried out in pleasure. He set the sacred stones on the altar of pleasure and turning, took her into his arms. Their eyes met and he smiled. With one last deep kiss, he felt her fade away into the mist. He retrieved the sacred stones and walking over to where his clothing lay in a pile on the cobbled road, picked up his satchel and put the stones in it.

He dressed slowly, and when he was once again fully clothed, he started walking along the cobbled path. With each step he took, the myludium night sky flashed with rich, vibrant colors. A portal opened before him, and he stepped in. Once again, he felt the pleasure pain as if his body and soul were being torn asunder. The colors faded slowly as the pleasure-pain subsided, and he found himself sitting in a chair at his desk. He let out a deep breath and removing the goggles, let them slip to the floor.

He sat there a moment, catching his breath, when he realized that someone was knocking at his door. It took him another minute to get up, and rubbing a hand down his cock to adjust himself, he made his way to the door.

"Fucking money hungry bastards," he mumbled as he flung the door open.

It was on the tip of his tongue to tell whoever it was to fuck off, but the words never made it past his lips.

There, before him, stood Kyra, the beautiful black warrior in his fantasy, and as he stood there speechless, she smiled at him and his heart stopped cold.

"Hello," she said, her voice soft and silky. "I was wondering if perhaps you could help us."

"Us?" he asked after he managed to get his breath back and his heart beating again.

The redheaded vixen from the game stepped into the doorway and he could only say, "Holy fuck!"

She ran her green eyes up and down the length of him and said on a smile, "Perhaps. We could give you a nice good fuck for helping us out. What do you think Shelby?"

Shelby laughed softly and nodding, ran her finger down the bulge in his pants, teasing him. "Perhaps, we could Toni."

Beneath her finger, his cock grew hard, straining against his zipper. "What do you need help with? I am always available to help ladies in distress."

He moved into the hall, closed the door

behind him and followed them to their apartment. He took the opportunity to get a glimpse of their asses and thought that both of them had a nice one indeed. Both of them looked pretty damn hot in those tight little shorts that hugged their ass nicely, showing off the nice round curve of their butt cheeks. They had fine legs too: long, lean, and silky smooth.

The best view though was watching them walk up the stairs. He got a good look at those two fine asses and would bet another weeks pay that they were just daring him to rip those shorts off and have his way with them.

Thinking about doing just that, he nearly stumbled on the stairs, and the jolt of almost falling knocked him back to reality. Laughing, they climbed the last stair and turned, heading down the hall. He went eagerly, though as he walked down the hall; he felt strangely out of place. He had been on this floor only once before, but he could have sworn there were just two apartments—two apartments per floor, just like the floor he was on. But now, there were three.

Opening the door at the end of the hall, the ladies walked in and he hesitated for just a moment, as he told himself that he had to be mistaken. He shook his head. "Don't blow this Johnny boy," he mumbled to himself and stepped over the threshold.

He took a quick look around, but it looked like his cheap-ass apartment, with the only difference being that they had spruced it up with girlie things. There were fancy pillows, lace curtains, and a nice Asian rug covering the floor. They had knick-knacks lining the walls and a bookshelf crammed with books, CD's, and DVD's. And over in one corner was a desk with a nice sound system and desktop.

Nodding, he said, "Nice place you got here."

Shelby walked to the small kitchen and opening the fridge, pulled out several cans of beer. She came back into the living room and offered him one. "Drink?"

He took the can and popped the top, taking a long swallow. Shelby gave the other can to Toni, and after opening it, she sat in one of the plush chairs by the window. He eyed her sheepishly, smiling, as he went and sat beside her on the arm of the chair while Toni took a seat opposite in another chair.

"So, what do you need help with?" he asked, his eyes getting a good peak of the top of her tits. She wore a skimpy red halter-top that barely managed to cover them, but he wasn't about to complain. Her nipples were hard and pointed high and he reached over and gave one a flick with his finger. When she let out a slow sigh of pleasure, he gave the other one a twist.

Shelby set her drink down and reached up and pulled his mouth to hers. She invaded his mouth with her tongue and ran it along the edge of his teeth, darting it in and out. He could taste the beer she just drank and the taste of it, of her, had his cock growing hard. He shoved his hand inside her halter-top and pulled her tits out, squeezing them, twisting the nipple between his two fingers.

"Hey, don't start without me," Toni said as she came over and started to unbutton his shirt. Within seconds, she had his shirt off and was rubbing her hands on his chest, kissing his shoulder, his back, his chest.

He thought of the stone alter in his game and figured the couch would fit the bill as a replacement. So he stood, and bringing Shelby to her feet, he went to work getting her out of that halter-top and those tight shorts. After he had her naked and quivering beneath his hands, he went to work on getting Toni naked, his hands working quickly, expertly.

While he was busy undressing Toni, Shelby ran her hands inside the band of his trousers and, reaching his zipper, freed his swollen cock. He led them both to the couch and, lying down on it, watched in anticipation as Toni spread her milky white thighs and straddled his head.

He accepted her invitation and buried his face in her moist pussy.

She was more than ready for him. Her pussy was wet and warm and he licked, lapped, and lashed out against the lips swollen with need. "Oh yeah, baby, OH YEAH!" she screamed as he took the slippery flesh between his teeth. He pulled and sucked on the mouth of her womanhood that was guarded only by a thin strip of red curly pubic hair. Rocking back and forth against him, her moans of pleasure ringing in his ears, he let out a loud groan when Shelby cupped his balls and took his seven-inch steel blade deep into her mouth.

For several minutes, Shelby sucked his cock hard and fast and then positioned herself above it and took him inch by slow inch into her pussy. Together, the three of them moved as one, rocking the couch, bumping it up against the wall. With his hands on Toni's waist, Shelby reached around, grabbed Toni's small, rounded breasts, and began massaging them, her dark brown eyes locking on his.

"I know you like this baby girl," Shelby whispered against Toni's heated skin.

"Fuck yeah!" Toni yelled as her orgasm ripped through her leaving her weak and trembling. Sliding off of him, she kissed Shelby hard on the mouth.

With their lips locked, Shelby increased

her pace, and he matched her speed. Pleasure speared him, spreading from his groin to his toes, and in one final thrust, he exploded, catching Shelby when she collapsed against him, her body trembling from her release.

He ran a hand down her back, cupped her ass, and let out a satisfied laugh. Shelby continued to lay on top of him, her fingers making tiny circles in his chest hair. Toni got up and retrieved her beer and then returned to take a seat on the floor beside them. For several minutes, they stayed that way, silent, the smell of sex ripe in the room.

Then on a chuckle, he asked, "What was it you needed help with?" Both women looked at him and began to laugh. His eyes darted from one then to the other. "What's the joke?"

Still laughing, Shelby looked at him and replied, "You, silly boy." Getting up, she planted another kiss on Toni, then walked over to the desk in the corner.

He sat up and looked on as she fired up the PC on the desk. "Oh my fucking God!" he exclaimed. "No fucking way!"

Shelby picked up a set of goggles and twirled them on her fingers. Brows raised, she smiled knowingly at him. "Welcome back Lord Darius," she said, then tossed the goggles aside and ran over to him.

She jumped on top of him, laughing,

while Toni kissed him tenderly. As both women prepared him for round two, his last coherent thought was that some fantasies really do come true.

2 WIDOWS OF SPORT UNITE

I was in my favorite chair in the corner of the sun lounge and looked out onto the immaculately manicured lawn in front of me. The young spring sun seemed to dance and move, highlighting first one and then another area of my beautiful garden as the clouds passed across the sky. There was no denying that I was a lucky woman in so many ways. I had a gorgeous house, a successful husband and the freedom to choose how I spent my own days.

The truth was that I felt lonely and lacking in purpose and worth. I realized that I needed to create more of a life for myself and find some friends of my own who I wanted to spend time with. Our social life was stereotypically suburban. We dined with the people we had to in order to retain our social status, and Graham's colleagues and associates from the gold club. Our evenings, while perfectly pleasant, felt manufactured and without genuine joviality. My days were empty. Graham worked hard and late and he was out of town regularly. We employed a cleaner so there was little to do around the house except for tending to the garden, a pleasure I refused to relinquish. I exercised every morning but that was where my own hobbies seemed to stop.

A couple of birds were splashing about in the pond at the bottom of the garden. They seemed playful and carefree. Watching their quirky games, I resolved to create a more fulfilling existence for myself. Now, I just needed to figure out where to start.

Although I wasn't always the biggest fan of the golf club, I did pay my membership, and it was nearby and in a lovely setting. I decided to take my laptop down there for a coffee and start doing some research. The change of scenery would do me good.

Sitting at my table outside the club, I flicked though some websites of local interest groups and contemplated what sort of things would appeal to my need for fulfillment. The coffee was good here and a pot of it shared the table with my computer. Taking a sip and looking around me, I noticed Lacey waving in my direction.

Lacey was married to one of my husband's colleagues. From memory, she was 29 or 30. A good 15 years younger than Walter at any rate. She wasn't approved of by everyone in the circle, but I personally found her younger, more independent style to be a refreshing change from the myriad of social convention that the more mature crowd had become so bogged down with. I waved back to her and she came over to my table.

"Mind if I take a seat? I've been trailing round the course after people all morning. I'm shattered!"

"Not at all. Please do!" I replied, smiling.

It might be an awful cliché, but Lacey had one of those smiles that brought a real sparkle to any situation. Her naturally blonde hair was cropped in a fashionable, elfin way that really suited her but would look dreadful on many. It framed her delicate yet confident features perfectly. It was no wonder that Walter adored her so fervently, but I wasn't sure what she saw in him! As far as I was concerned, he was a bit of a bore, worked far too hard, and looked every day of the fifteen years he had on his wife.

Still, it wasn't for me to judge or even care, so I washed such thoughts from my head and focused on what the younger girl had to say.

"It's unusual to see you down here on your own and during the day," tinkled Lacey, "Is Graham out on the course? I assumed he'd be on this overnight business trip with Walter."

"Yes, he's with Walter. I was going stir crazy in the house on my own so I decided to get out for a bit."

"It's easy to do, isn't it? Go stir crazy, I mean. Walter does insist that I don't work and it's frustrating sometimes. I thought my fundraising gigs would be enough to keep me busy when we first married, but I still find myself with time on my hands. It's actually quite lonely most of the time."

Lacey's honesty astonished me slightly. Only that morning, I'd finally admitted to myself that I was lonely and bored. I had been for years, but it had taken until now to start to acknowledge and act on it. Here was this girl, a good ten years or so younger than me, freely talking about a personal situation to me with no indication of shame or embarrassment. I was surprised to find myself opening up to her in response.

"Tell me about it. I'm pretty sure that, other than a bit of baking, the gym and the odd salon appointment, I actually do nothing. Hence the laptop—I've decided I need to stop wasting my life and start enjoying it!"

"Well, I guess there must be something to be said for the gym and salon appointments. You're looking incredible, Ruth!"

I blushed slightly.

"Thanks, Lacey. I want to grow old gracefully and figured that the best way was to keep in shape."

Admittedly, she was right. I was naturally tall and slender with olive skin and shiny, thick black hair. But it was Graham's money and my empty life that kept me in the gym and having the salon treatments that maintained my sultry, high-maintenance appearance.

"Well it's working. And less of the old! So I'm at a loose end as well. Why don't we have a bite of lunch and a glass of wine? It's not like we have anything else to do with the corporate bores of the century away on their trip!"

"Why not," I mused. "It would be nice to have some company, and a drop of Sauvignon Blanc would go down a treat."

Lacey disappeared inside the clubhouse to procure the wine and a couple of menus, and I found myself contemplating my life again. My marriage wasn't bad and I loved Graham, but I was starting to realize that we'd become too comfortable. Other than the required social functions, we spent very little time in the same room these days, even when he was home. I couldn't remember the last time we showed any genuine affection towards each other. My expectations of wild, racy sex and passionate embraces had naturally trailed off during our 15 years of marriage, but surely some sex at 40 wasn't unheard of?

Sitting on the terrace of the golf club summoned the memory of one particular day, when, still in the heady heights of our late twenties and the first few years of our relationship, Graham and I had made love right here on the grounds of the course. There'd been a local tournament on that day and Graham wasn't playing. We'd taken a picnic and a blanket down to the club and found a place to sit under the trees and drink in the atmosphere before heading into the clubhouse for the post-tournament social later in the day.

The weather hadn't been as nice as forecast and it seemed to keep many of the spectators at bay. We'd settled ourselves near the 18th hole, and nobody else was there yet. It would be a good hour or so before the first golfers trickled up, and we pretty much had the place to ourselves. Giggling about some of the older members of the club, Graham had suddenly turned to me and put his glass down onto the lid of the picnic box. Before I'd had time to register his intentions, he was kissing me fiercely. My whole body seemed to set alight instantly, the shudders running through my chest and taking my breath away. "This man wants me so badly!" I remember thinking. And that he did.

My young, fertile libido wanted him back, and I wasted no time in succumbing to his desires, allowing him to push me back down onto the blanket and firmly run his hands up my skirt, over my tits and through my long, thick hair.

"God woman, you're hot for it aren't you? Admit it; you want my cock inside you, don't you?" I liked it hard and dirty. I didn't always come that way, but I didn't need to. I got my kicks from the noises and faces that portrayed my husband's raw urgency and desperation. He was very well endowed (I also remember our wedding night, when I'd been terrified at the size of his cock. He didn't know that I had slept with someone else before him, and so I couldn't admit that his hard dick was twice the size I'd been used to, but my cunt was already drenched and ready for him. He slid my panties down, marveling at the wet trail that was revealed. By not touching my pussy first, Graham increased the impact that the first thrust had on my body.

Crying out, I realized I needed to stifle my vocals. I liked to make noise, but now was not the time or place. This was a smart club and getting caught would not just lose us our membership, it would damage my husband's career and our livelihood. That didn't seem to bother him though, as he continued to push inside me. His hips seemed to be completely out of his control as they pressed me hard into the solid ground beneath and the look on his face was animal. I was getting a huge kick out of submitting to his sudden dominance, and his knowledge of this spurred him to fuck me deeper, harder and faster. He came so hard that his tight buttocks continued to shake as his cock leapt and twitched inside my young twat. Unbelievably, the lascivious look in his eyes and the pressure of his groin against my clit prompted me to climax.

"Oh baby, really? That's amazing!" He panted. "We should never stop doing this. We are so damn intense when we screw. Let's promise never to stop fucking."

I'd agreed, of course, and was high on what we had. Sadly, I realized now, that pact had long evaporated, and we were sexually distanced from each other. The recollection of our steamy encounter only served to compound this, and I realized that over 18 months had passed since our last, perfunctory attempt to become pregnant. Could it be that part of my unhappiness was due to sexual frustration?

I quickly calmed myself down and

pasted on a calm smile as I saw Lacey returning to the table with a waiter in tow. He was carrying an ice bucket and our menus.

"Sorry—I hope you don't think I'm leading you astray," Lacey smiled apologetically, "the barman convinced me that it was better value to take the bottle and I was inclined to agree with him."

I couldn't help but chuckle to myself at Lacey's innocence. She appeared completely unaware of the effect she had on all the men in this place. They became enchanted with her unusual but breathtaking looks, azure eyes, and captivating smile. Each and every one of them seemed convinced that they would be the guy to rescue the girl from her unsuitable husband.

"Even if you were, I wouldn't object. Today seems like a day to be led astray. I've been bored for too long!" I declared emphatically.

"Great—in that case let's tuck in."

The wine was cool and crisp and my companion was entertaining. We ordered salads and chatted about the perils of being a stay at home wife. Lacey explained that she got heavily involved in fundraising for a couple of the local charities, but that she was growing tired of the gaps in her days and the lack of real friends. If she was unhappy with Walter, she didn't allude to it and I didn't pry. If truth be told, I was very slightly in awe of this woman. The more I got talking to her, the more intriguing she became. She was wearing cotton, 1950s-style sundress. It accented her petite figure beautifully, and I couldn't help but notice how womanly her figure was, despite being so small. Her breasts weren't large as such, though significantly larger than my own, but perfectly round and soft looking. They were balanced out by her hips and the dress emphasized her tiny waist. It was no wonder she had so many admirers.

Right now, it seemed like I'd never have sex again. Every human form seemed to be rubbing salt into the wound. I found myself wondering how Lacey would look without the dress, what the touch of a woman would be like. I imagined it to be sensual, delicate and arousing. I imagined the alabaster skin of her limbs contrasting against my own olive body. Realizing how inappropriate my thoughts were becoming, I checked myself suddenly and poured a glass of water to weaken the effect of the wine.

"So I was thinking," began Lacey, "that maybe we should meet up later in the week. Go to the cinema or something to get us out the house. When Walter and Graham aren't working, they're usually to be found playing golf or watching football.

Maybe it's time for us to have a bit of leisure time and fun ourselves!"

"That would be lovely," I agreed. "There's a film on at the plaza that I've been wanting to see for a couple of weeks. They have a matinee on Thursday afternoons if you're free."

Lacey checked her diary and confirmed that she was, and we agreed to meet at a café over the road from the cinema for a light lunch before the film. We paid the bill and went our separate ways. I needed a strong coffee and a lie down. The wine had gone right to my head!

My Prada bag and house keys had been dumped on the kitchen table, and I now lay sprawled out on the sofa with a cup of coffee, the radio murmuring in the background, and a copy of a fairly trashy romance novel I'd picked up a few days before. I felt happier for having made social plans of my own and right now the absence of responsibility in my life felt like a blessing rather than a chore. The lunchtime drinking had compromised my ability to concentrate, however, and I must have read the same sentence at least six or seven times.

Putting the book down on the table beside me, I laid back and closed my eyes.

I wanted sex. I couldn't believe I hadn't realized before. But Hell, even the wife of my husband's best friend had been looking good to me at lunchtime and I'd never been even slightly bi-curious. Things must be bad! I began to consider my chances of tempting Graham on his return from business the following day. As I lazily contemplated how it would feel to have my pussy stroked after all these months, I realized my hand had fallen to my small but still firm breast and begun to idly caress it. The lunchtime Sauvignon was having an aphrodisiac effect and I suddenly realized that, Graham or no Graham, I could still cum if I wanted to. I'd thought that my libido and sense of desire had died along with my sex life, but it appeared I was wrong. My hand made its way down to my stomach and then down beneath my waistband. I tentatively brushed my finger over the mound beneath by functional white cotton briefs and shuddered. I was about to do something that I hadn't done since I was a young woman.

I thought back to that day at the golf club with Graham as I slipped my hand under my panties and gasped at the feeling of flesh against my swollen clitoris. My fingers started to massage and probe at the soft folds of my womanhood as I fantasized about him holding me down so hard and fucking me so hungrily. I pictured his dirty, bawdy grin and the excitement in his eyes. I tried to feel his thick cock entering my dripping pussy, but it only served to frustrate me. Nothing I could do here, alone, could possibly re-create that feeling.

My hand didn't stop working, however, and I was surprised when my thoughts drifted from my husband to Lacey. I thought about how it would feel to touch my cheek across her pale, inviting bosom and feel her hand trace up the outside of my thigh as she leaned in to kiss me with those blossom-like lips. Before I had time to stop myself, I was imagining her mouth gently and expertly working my wanting clit while she murmured that she'd always fantasized about making a woman cum. My fingers pressed harder and with increased pace. My left hand was cupping my own breast tightly and my hips began to buck gently as the sweet sensation of orgasm started to rack my body. Words cannot describe how this felt. If you've gone 18 months without cumming, you'll know what I mean.

I reached over to the coffee table and picked up my phone.

Graham—hope the trip is going well. Let's go out for dinner when you're back tomorrow night. Just the two of us.

The text message sent, I went upstairs

to have a shower and bring myself around a bit.

Graham's reply was irritating but completely expected. There was a cup match tomorrow night, and he'd already arranged to watch it on the TV down at the club with Walter and some of the others. Typical. I supposed it served me right for being naïve enough to think that a text was all it took to rekindle the spark in your marriage. Just as I was about to head into the garden, my phone beeped again.

Can't believe it. Walter's ditched me tomorrow night to go and watch the game. Have an invitation a new bar opening with free champagne and canapés. Don't suppose you fancy keeping me company? Lacey xxx

My first reaction to this was horror and guilt, then I realized that Lacey would obviously have no idea that she'd been featured in my fantasy earlier, and why should she. Goodness, I'd read enough Nancy Friday when I was younger to know that there was nothing sinister about the odd fantasy. Instead, Lacey was providing me with an escape route from another dull evening as a sports widow. I typed out a response, accepting her invitation and thanking her for thinking of me.

I had plenty of clothes and could have bought more had I wanted to, but getting ready for the evening at the bar was proving more difficult than usual. Was I trying to dress for Lacey or was I simply concerned that her youth and unusual tastes would make me look dull and unimaginative at the bar? Either way, I needed to make a decision—she was due to pick me up in 15 minutes. I flicked through the vast rail of clothes once more and decided on an old faithful that I hadn't worn for years. It had lost favor when Graham pointed out that it might be a bit short for a woman of my age. That had caused a battle!

Slipping it on I realized it was fine and actually quite classy. Yes, it was a shorter than the average skirt, but I had good legs and I slipped on a pair of sheer, barely black stockings to match. A few touch-ups to my make-up, and I was ready to go.

Lacey appeared at the door in a cloud of heady scent, a perfume so intoxicating that it threw me for a moment. Her incredible figure was clad in some sort of kooky vintage number in silver and supported by a cute pair of heels. She looked both stunning and effortless though rather than knowing it, she seemed genuine as she gushed about how I looked. She stated that we were clearly the winners and would be having a much better night than the men. I concurred, and we hopped into the car where Lacey's driver was waiting patiently.

Wow! What a spectacle lay before us when we pulled up to the bar. It certainly seemed to be the hub for any young, rich talent in the area. Toned, charismatic young men leaned casually on the counters and chatted to tiny, manicured waifs with big eyes and perfectly straightened hair. Sexual tension hung in the thick air like the first scent of pollen after spring rain. It was intoxicating and overwhelming at the same time. I was fascinated, but I needed champagne, and fast, if I stood any chance of feeling at ease here.

Lacey's eyes were lit up and twinkling more than ever before as we made our way inside to seek out a drink. Before we had a chance to get our bearings and find the bar, a waistcoat-clad server was in front of us, offering champagne or cocktails from a silver tray. We gratefully accepted our glasses of fizz and settled in a spot where we could people watch and chat. Though the bar was busy and full to bursting, it was a pleasant ambience and we were still able to hear ourselves think and maintain a conversation without having to shout at each other. I couldn't believe how indulgent it felt to be out, of my own accord, without my husband. It was amazing!

Graham hadn't so much as batted an eyelid when he came home, probably, because he was so preoccupied with getting back out the door as quickly as possible. His being away so much was one thing; it was the way I didn't seem to exist when he was at home that I found so hurtful and frustrating. Still, this wasn't the time or place to get down about it. I was dolled up, drinking champagne and surrounded by beautiful people. Beautiful people that I could see Lacey was quite entranced by. This surprised me. She was young and beautiful herself, she fit right in, and I didn't expect this to be as much of a culture shock and thrill for her as it was for me.

"You OK Lacey?" I asked.

"Sure—just drooling over this bunch!" Lacey answered cheekily, that twinkle haunting me yet again. This woman seemed to have a hold over me. Everything about her seemed perfect. I wanted to touch her. Her porcelain skin and moist pink mouth looked so soft and inviting. Never before had a woman conjured up this strange sense of intrigue within me. It was as if she was a witch who had cast a spell.

"I'll be honest with you, Ruth. I'm bored. Walter is a good guy. I don't expect people to understand our marriage. Lord, I know everyone speculates down at the club…" I cringed inwardly at these words. I had been one of those people speculating. "But he's a good man. I didn't marry him for his money as everyone makes out, but it is more complicated than people realize. He's a LOT older than me and I miss sex."

"Tell me about it," I chimed in, "I can't remember the last time Graham and I slept together. But then again, I'm a fair bit older than you!"

My mind was flicking back to the day before as we had this conversation, slightly more risqué than those we'd had before. I remembered how Lacey had suddenly taken over my fantasy, and the intensity of the resulting orgasm.

"I want hot, crazy, outta control sex." The younger girl continued, "I see these people here. These people who are my age. They're on fire with it. You can see passion and potential and sexual excitement exploding from every one of them. I just want someone to remind me how that electricity feels. What it's like to finally get down to it after a long build up and flirtation. But I can't have it. I couldn't do it to Walter. I know he'd turn a blind eye, but I know it would kill him if he thought, let alone knew, that I'd been with another man. It would emasculate him."

My heart went out to the younger girl as she looked up from her drink, and I caught the sadness she was trying to keep from her face. I knew how she felt. She was exceptionally attractive, feisty, and emotional. This was a girl who had men vying for her affections wherever she went but, for reasons she evidently didn't want to discuss, was bound to a man who couldn't give her what she so badly wanted. To be touched and loved, physically and hungrily. She wanted to feel like a woman her age should. Not just to be wanted, but to be irresistible. She felt just like me.

I instinctively reached out my hand to comfort her, not thinking about the effect this may have on my rapidly developing crush. As we stood, so close together in the busy bar, I reached my arm around her and looked into her eyes. An almighty surge of electricity seemed to pass through my body, and I fought to keep it to one side and focus on being comforting rather than lustful.

"Hey," I comforted, "Don't get upset. It's quite common, you know. Walter obviously adores you. I'm not entirely sure Graham even remembers I exist these days. That's one of the reasons I'm so grateful to you for inviting me here tonight and for the cinema trip tomorrow. The reason I was at the club yesterday is because I'm going crazy at home. Rattling around with nothing to do. I've been missing any sort of human contact that is real. Making small talk over cocktails with Graham's colleagues or golfing buddies doesn't count!"

"Well then, we'd better have a great night then hadn't we!" Lacey's mood seemed to have been buoyed suddenly, and she grabbed a couple more glasses from a passing waiter, thrust one at me and grinned wickedly. "Let's have another, then dance. Or talk to strangers. Or both!"

"Sounds good to me!" We drank our champagne quickly and headed over to the dance floor.

It was obvious that I wasn't the only one beguiled by Lacey's inherent sex appeal. A stream of guys made their way over to our corner of the floor, dancing up close and hoping it would be enough to get them noticed. One or two were bolder and tried a line on her, but simply got laughed off. Lacey had said that she wanted to talk to strangers, but it seemed she was just as happy dancing and keeping to ourselves. I sneaked glances at her frequently. Her vintage dress enclosed her delicate yet curvaceous form perfectly and the creamy hint of cleavage emerging from its neckline was accentuated as she gently moved and twisted her shoulders in time with the music. I felt my pussy start to throb as I let my imagination run away with me again. As I danced to the slow, trendy music, I lost all concept of what was around me and was completely enveloped in my saucy private daydream.

"I'm sorry, I'm a lesbian. But if I were straight, you'd definitely be my type." The sound of Lacey's voice uttering these words brought me back to the bar with a sharp, disbelieving jolt. The guy smiled and left, looking slightly dejected for all of about 5 seconds before he spotted his next target.

"What was that?" I asked Lacey, astonished.

"A little trick I've learned. I don't want to be tempted, and I discovered a while ago that a lot of these men will be more persistent if I say I'm married," she laughed.

Of course that was it. How could I be stupid enough to let my heart leap? She's already said she couldn't bear to hurt Walter, and she was obviously straight. As was I. She seemed to be the exception to my rule, but it was never going to happen. Maybe this friendship wasn't going to work after all. Still, I was out and enjoying myself rather than sitting at home alone while Graham drank in the golf club, so it couldn't be that bad.

"Here, watch this." Lacey nodded her head subtly in the direction of six foot of tall, dark, and handsome making his way over to our spot on the dance floor. He was clearly hot on the blonde girl's trail and his beeline was directly for us. Before I knew what was happening, Lacey was moving her cool, soft hands up to the back of my neck and pressing those rounded, perfect tits I'd been fantasizing about right into my own. The feeling was so delectable I thought my legs would give way, or, worse still, that I'd give myself away. Before I had time to worry about that, she was pressing her delicate mouth into mine and kissing me. It felt unlike anything I'd ever known. Fireworks were going off inside me, the hairs were standing on end where she was touching my neck, and I felt my panties soaking almost instantly.

Lacey looked a little odd as she pulled away, and I was terrified she'd noticed my attraction to her. I'd spoilt everything, yet never wanted her so badly.

"See, nowhere to be seen!" Lacey tried to breeze, but her tone was still a little uncomfortable. I'd screwed up, but it was too late to do anything about it. We had one final drink before calling her driver, who dropped me home on their way.

I was nervous as I got ready to meet Lacey for lunch before our cinema outing. She'd kissed me, only to prove a point, but it was me who had reacted. I didn't know whether I should feel or show remorse for that or not. Her awkwardness could be attributed the fact she realized that I may not have been comfortable with her actions. Either way, I was really hoping it didn't cast an uncomfortable shadow over our afternoon together.

Graham had arrived home an hour after me the night before. I was horny and tried to pluck up the courage to initiate sex for the first time in forever, but he clearly wasn't interested or capable. I didn't persist, wishing to save myself the embarrassment, so instead went upstairs and drew myself a bath. It was there, soaking in the tub, that I began to run my hands over my wet skin and take myself back to the moment with Lacey in the bar.

The thought of her soft lips on mine and the way her breasts had pushed up so close to mine that I could feel our hardened nipples making contact through the fabric of our clothes served to turn me on quickly. I leaned back, resting my head on the back of the bathtub whilst one hand ran over my thigh and the other very gently traced my clit and the soft folds of my pussy. I needed to be able to feel my clit being touched by someone or something else. I needed to believe that someone was getting me off and taking pleasure in doing so.

I reached over to the shower faucet and lifted it down from its hook. Our tub was large and deep and I'd had an idea. Switching the faucet on, I leaned back again and began to let the jet of water tantalize my clit. It felt unbelievable, and I thought of Lacey as the water did its work. The way her hips moved when she danced. The way her eyes sparkled in a mischievous sort of way. You could tell she'd be a demon lover—passionate, intense, and dirty when she wanted to be. I grabbed my own ass as I pictured her getting really worked up filthy. This pushed my clit closer to the jet from the shower, increasing the pressure. All of a sudden, I was moaning, over and over, as the orgasm cascaded through my body. Even more intense than the day before.

Now I had to put those thoughts behind me, so as not to pounce on Lacey the moment we got to the restaurant. That would not be acceptable! I dressed much more casually than the night before, but picking a long, clingy top and skinny jeans that I knew showed off my figure. Finishing the look off with a pair of heeled boots, I decided I'd do.

A last minute panic grabbed me as I was about to head out of the door. Maybe I should feign illness and call it off? I laughed to myself as I realized what I was thinking. Three days ago I'd been lonely, bored, and utterly miserable of my meaningless existence. Now I had excitement, dilemmas, and company. What was I thinking? I walked down the front path with confidence and tried my best to push all feelings of confusion out of my head. It wasn't easy, and as I walked to the restaurant, I flicked between doubt, nerves, and fantasy. An exhausting combination as it happened, and I decided I needed a strong coffee when I got to the restaurant; otherwise, I'd be falling asleep on Lacey's shoulder the moment the film started. Mmmmmm... Lacey's shoulder...

The sight of Lacey jolted me both awake and to my senses. She was sitting at a table on the terrace wearing yet another fabulous sundress (with even more cleavage this time, I couldn't help but notice) and one of those smiles that wipes away all concern. She was normal, breezy, and genuinely happy to see me. I relaxed, forgot all about the night before and ordered coffee while we studied the menu.

"I was thinking of just a salad or something because there's only an hour before the film starts," she said.

I agreed that this was the most sensible option and we placed our orders.

"Walter was back before me last night.

Apparently, the game wasn't that great." Lacey stated, casually.

"Really? Graham arrived a good hour after me. He must have stayed on at the club with some of the others. He was shattered and worse for wear when he came home. To be honest, I feel like I live alone these days!" As I said the words, I realized that this no longer saddened me. I seemed to have moved on from that time.

"Well, I think I know why. I don't know if it's my place Ruth, but since we've become closer, I feel like I need to tell you something." Lacey looked nervous, an emotion that the confident, outspoken woman had never displayed in my presence before. Suddenly, it was obvious.

"He's having an affair, isn't he? I can't believe I didn't realize sooner!"

"No, he's not. Well, not that I know of anyway. But he has told Walter that he feels the two of you have grown apart. I think he wants to separate. Walter says he sees it as setting you free. He feels you need a different life to the one he allows you to have, and I'm inclined to agree with him. Are you OK?"

I realized that Lacey was asking me the question because of the tears streaming down my face. She pulled me close to comfort me, holding my head so close to her breasts it was all I could do not to kiss her cleavage tenderly.

"I'm fine. I...I think I'm happy about it."
I was relieved, without a doubt. I knew
that my financial settlement would be
generous, but finally I could move on with
my life. I would be sad to see Graham go,
but we had nothing in common anymore.
Our marriage had fizzled away, and I
didn't have the energy or the inclination to
salvage it.

The food arrived and we ate, talking
about marriage and relationships and the
difficulties of sustaining them. As we were
having this semi-serious conversation, my
thoughts kept wandering to the night
before. I couldn't stop conjuring up the
memories of my first human touch in such
a long time. I wasn't sure any more if it
was Lacey that had sparked these, or just
the fact that I'd been craving someone's
attraction. To know that somebody wanted
me and to feel the un-paralleled sensation
of being caressed, turned on and then
fucked. It was as I thought this that Lacey
suddenly piped up with a change in topic.

"Do you mind missing the film?" She
asked. "I'd like to talk to you about
something, but it probably requires some
time and it definitely calls for something
stronger than coffee!"

I was intrigued and enjoying her
company and so agreed vehemently. She
ordered wine from the waiter and I let her
continue the previous topic. Whatever it

was she obviously felt the need for Dutch courage and given that I was slightly concerned she was going to confront me for kissing her back last night, I was happy to delay the conversation for as long as possible. Lacey could certainly put the drink away, however, and I was surprised upon realizing that we'd polished off the bottle already.

"Come back to mine," she said. "I have plenty to drink there and the garden is lovely to sit out in this time of year. Walter's away again and I'd welcome the company."

I couldn't have said no to this woman, even if I'd wanted to. This was panning out to be an odd afternoon (huge understatement!) and something made it impossible for me to voluntarily leave this woman's company. I was enchanted.

I'd been to Lacey's house many times for dinner parties led by Walter for the golf and/or work crew. It was lovely and, to be honest, very similar to our house. I pushed the thoughts of what would happen at our house away. I'd deal with that tonight. This afternoon was for denial!

We settled in the garden with a bottle of sparkling wine. Lacey was a rebel and had brought a blanket out so we could lie, carefree, on the grass rather than sit on their expensive patio furniture. It was liberating to throw off our shoes and just be normal instead of bowing down to social convention.

"I wanted to kiss you yesterday," Lacey announced, suddenly breaking the silence and prompting me to all but choke on my drink. She didn't stop there. "You're stunning, but vulnerable too. I can't stop thinking about you. In fact, I think I may have lured you here with an ulterior motive." If I couldn't quite believe this news, I didn't have time to try.

The object of my sexual fantasies for the last few days was stroking my face and kissing me again. This time it wasn't for show, there wasn't anybody to show. The electric shock feelings were back, this time stronger than ever because I could let them flood through me. This was it; my fantasy was going to become a reality! But then she suddenly pulled back, shattering my moment of euphoria.

"I'm sorry, I'm sorry. I don't know what's wrong with me at the moment. Please, forgive me." Suddenly, my years and maturity took over me, and it was with an adult confidence I was able to reassure her, trying my hardest to make sure that whatever happened next was the right thing.

"Lacey, it's OK. I think we've both been

lonely and, to be honest, I've been having similar thoughts. I've never been with a woman before, but there's something about you that I find utterly intoxicating. When you kissed me last night, I honestly thought I'd died and gone to heaven. Then I realized you were putting on a show and I was terrified that you'd noticed how aroused I was!" I was no longer nervous, and my confession was heartfelt. Lacey looked both relieved and confused, so I went on. The wine had gone to my head, but it was the strength of my desire to spend the afternoon with Lacey on this lawn, naked, that spurred me on the most.

I began to tell her about how I'd pleasured myself and cum for the first and then second time in well over a year, all whilst imagining it was her touch I could feel on my desperate pussy. I told her how I'd spent most of lunchtime today trying not to stare at her magnificent tits and how I'd almost kissed them when she'd been comforting me. Lacey's eyes widened at first, then began to light up more than ever before. That naughty look was back and she beckoned me towards her.

"Like this, you mean?" She whispered as she pulled down my own top and began to brush and kiss the tops of my breasts with her lips.

"Yes, yes. Oh my God, just like that." I started to run my hands over her body, settling them on her beautifully curved breasts. One of my hands settled on her naked cleavage as it rose up and down above the neckline of her dress, the other cupped underneath. They were even bigger and firmer than they looked, and my pussy was throbbing violently with anticipation.

"You say you've never been with a woman. Well, I have. Many times in fact. I'd like to show you what I learnt." I genuinely thought I might cum just listening to Lacey speak. I felt like I was dreaming, but as I felt her hands gently easing down my jeans, I knew that this was so much better than a dream could ever be. Her head was down between my legs; right there out on the grass lawn behind the house she shared with her husband. She'd pulled off my top and exposed my braless tits to the warm, exciting air. She kissed and teased my taut, flat stomach with her lips and tongue as her fingers explored my pubis over the silk of my panties. She circled around my clit and teased me until I thought I might cry out with frustration. Just when I thought she might venture inside my panties, she pulled back from me yet again.

I was glad she did, though, as it transpired, she had done so to free herself from the confines of her sundress. Pulling over her head, I got a full frontal view of the body I'd been picturing last night as I'd masturbated in the bathtub. Her hips and breasts were so full and womanly, but her frame was tiny and her waist so defined and small. She looked so young and innocent, yet here she was working me like an expert.

She rolled right up to me so that our bodies, devoid of all clothing except our panties, were pressed up close to each other. I could feel her breathing matching mine exactly, and as her clit grazed mine, I had to bite my lip to stop me alerting the neighbors to my ecstasy.

"Feel me," commanded Lacey. "I'm so wet." And that was an understatement. I could feel the warmth of her juices through her panties. I pushed my fingers beneath the fabric and started, for the very first time, to gently stimulate another woman's clitoris.

"You first," she all but moaned. "I need to see you cum. I'm picturing you on your sofa and in the bath, all the while thinking of me. Now I need to see it for myself."

With that, the horny young girl dropped down and deftly slid my panties off as she did so. Her head fell to my crotch and I couldn't stop myself from moaning this time. If her lips had felt soft and irresistible on mine, it was nothing compared to the feeling of them gently sucking my aching clit. She paused for a moment.

"Tell me again," she whispered. "Tell me about your fantasy while I lick your pussy. I want to hear it. I'm going to make it a reality."

And so I began to quietly recount the tale. The pace at which she was sucking and licking my throbbing slit increased in time with the pace of my story. As I began to build up to my climax, I knew I was going to cum again at the same moment. So long had passed since I'd had any sex, either alone or with someone else, and now I was recounting a personal, dirty tale of getting myself off on the sofa while another woman lapped hungrily and urgently at my clit. I had never, ever been this aroused and as I started to cry out, no longer caring about who could hear, I knew that I'd never climaxed like this before either. It came in wave upon wave upon wave. I could barely breathe and I realized that tears of ecstasy were streaming down my face. Here I was, at forty years old, previously sure my sexual peak had passed, having just found out that my marriage was ending, lying on my back and experiencing pleasure I'd never dreamed of. And as I rolled Lacey over to return the favor, I knew that this was just going to get better and better.

3 SWINGING HIGH

John and Liz were high on life. Their honeymoon was proving to be just what they needed after the months of stress leading up to their beautiful wedding. Four days in and they were out on the town, just finishing a slap up meal and about to head over the road to a cocktail bar they'd had their eyes on. They'd had loads of recommendations for beach resorts and paradise islands given to them, but they hadn't fancied it for some reason. The long flights and nothing to do but lay about didn't appeal to the couple's sense of adventure. Eventually, they'd settled on a city tour of Europe. It might not seem exotic to many, but there were so many places they'd not visited and with three weeks to do it, the timing was perfect.

They'd landed in Prague that morning after a few romantic days in Paris and already loved its eccentricities and cheap booze! Liz looked at her new hubby and smiled.

"Let's hit the cocktails! I'm in the mood for some fun."

"Great plan babe," John replied, "let's do it."

The mojitos were to die for and the newlyweds were feeling a little merry. Killer tunes had been belting out from the bar's sound system all night, and they were getting hot and sweaty on the dance floor. Liz noted how much easier it was to let your hair down when you didn't know anybody. She wasn't particularly self-conscious. Aesthetically, she knew she was attractive. Her tall slim frame was topped by a mass of shiny auburn hair, green eyes, and a wicked smile. John worshipped her, and she was the life and soul of any number of parties. But this was different. She was anonymous to all but John on this trip, and it was doing her the world of good.

The smile on John's face as he lost himself in the music indicated that he felt the same. It felt like he had it all. Stopping for a second to drink in the vision of his wife before him, tossing her hair back over her shoulder and moving her hips alluringly in time with the beat, he knew he wanted to take her to bed for the second time that day. They'd eaten breakfast and had to go straight back up to their room, on account of the fact that Liz had been stroking his thigh with her foot under the tablecloth. He'd gulped his eggs down at lightning speed with a huge boner. As a result, their coupling had been brief but intense once he'd got her upstairs and stripped off. Now he wanted another go, but this time he vowed to take more time over it. He was going to tease her to the point of frustration.

Liz saw John looking over at her and caught the twinkle in his eye. She grabbed his hands, pulling him towards her and back onto the dance floor, and kissed him as they moved.

"You look amazing," John told her, "really great. I love being married to you, especially when it means episodes like this morning!"

"There's plenty more where that came from," assured Liz, with a suggestive twinkle in her eye. They were both getting turned on again. Lost in the sea of people on the floor, they danced closely together, kissing passionately and grinding together.

Liz was liberated and in love. John was tracing the curves of her body through the loose silk shirt she was wearing, and a few minutes later, she was guiding him out of the bar and back towards their hotel. Stopping him on the street she turned and kissed him again, giving him a flavor of what was to come.

Giggling, they half walked and half ran, hand in hand, through the hotel reception and into the elevator. Being the only two in there, they began kissing and groping as soon as the doors closed, only springing apart as they arrived on their floor.

As they fell into their room, Liz began pulling at John's shirt in a bid to free him from it.

"No, no, no, not yet!" John exclaimed. "I'm going to make you wait for it tonight."

Frustrated but titilated at the thought, Liz conceded and allowed her husband to lie her down on the bed and take his time appreciating every inch of her. John's fingers caressed her face and neck and moved to trace the lines of her body over her delicate clothing. She twitched and sighed in response to his touch. His deliberate approach was arousing each tiny portion of her skin, and she could feel warm juices escaping from her cunt and into her French panties.

Pushing her groin up into his firm, determined body, Liz began to make it known to her husband just how badly she needed to be fucked. She wasn't begging just yet, but it wasn't going to be long before her frustration reached its pinnacle. She kissed and bit at his lips and broad shoulders in the hope that he too would be unable to wait as a result.

John continued to stay strong however, and with her nipples erect to the point of pain and her neat pussy screaming for attention, Liz decided it was time for a more direct approach. His thick cock was already twitching and pushing under his thin linen trousers, so with one swift movement, Liz tugged at the elastic waistband and freed him from their confines. Her husband stopped what he was doing for a moment as he allowed his body to appreciate the wave of satisfaction that followed. It was at this point that Liz took her opportunity and, quick as a flash, moved her head down and ran her tongue over his sensitive balls.

John cried out with satisfaction. Though he'd tried to hide it, the extended foreplay had been frustrating him as much as it had her, and the sudden attention she was paying to his dick was not before time. She knew just how to handle him – he'd screwed other women before meeting Liz, but not one of them had quite managed to please him in the way she did. She started to slide her mouth down his throbbing shaft, pausing for a moment to flick her tongue round its glistening head, and John knew that this time was going to be no exception.

Using her hand and mouth simultaneously on her husband's perfect cock, Liz felt him move round the bed, and she realized she was about to be in for a real treat. John was about to reciprocate the oral attention he was getting.

"Hell yes!" exclaimed Liz in response to the 69, "my filthy boy's about to give as good as he gets!" She stopped short there – the moment his mouth fixed down onto her clit and sucked gently at it.

"Oh god John, your mouth really knows how to please my pussy. It was aching for you. I bet this looks hot!"

"It does. You'd love to watch this back on video, wouldn't you? Imagine we were being filmed, showing everyone else how it should be done!"

Liz could already feel the beginnings of her orgasm starting to build – she was thrusting her hips in and out in response to John's lips teasing her clit. The thrill of getting turned on in the bar had taken effect and the young woman knew she was in for an intense climax pretty soon. She responded by really starting to go for it on her husband's dick. She pumped her mouth up and down, running her hands first over his tightening balls and then grasping the base of his shaft as she sucked.

"Shit Liz, be careful. I'll be spunking in

your mouth any second if you carry on like that!"

His words were all it took. Liz screamed out in surprise as the waves of pleasure began rolling through her pussy and entire body. Her hips bucked and her cries were muffled as John shot his hot, salty come into the mouth that looked so sweet and delicate, but was capable of reducing him to this within seconds.

As the newlyweds lay panting and euphoric in their afterglow, they smiled at each other.

"Married life rocks!" John commented. "And being away makes me naughty. I feel like experimenting while we're here. It's time to live out some of those fantasies we're always talking about."

Liz was thrilled at this. The heady scent of sex that surrounded her seemed to make her braver.

"Let's look out a club for tomorrow night. See a 'special' show maybe. Something dirty. Nobody can catch us here. We can do what we want."

"Deal. Definitely a deal," grinned John, "I want to give you what you've always wanted."

Liz wasn't quite sure which part of "what she wanted" John was referring to, but she didn't ask. The uncertainty was thrilling in itself and she could tell John felt the same. His cock had started to twitch and harden for the third time that day, so she rolled over, straddled him, and rode him until they both came again.

They woke early the next day and headed down to breakfast to refuel after their exertions the night before. They chatted idly over breakfast about their plans for the day. It was decided that they'd get out and see some of the sights on their list and then head down to the river for a late lunch in the sun. Liz was secretly wondering whether the late lunch would lead to that club, as they'd talked about the night before. She didn't dare bring it up, for fear that it had just been John's peaking libido talking.

By the time they reached the terrace of the restaurant by the river, the couple was weary from walking and ready for some sustenance. They ordered starters, salads for main, and a bottle of sparkling wine on ice. The weather was hot and their selection suited the conditions. Liz beamed at John from underneath her sunglasses, and he took a moment to appreciate the beauty before him in the stunning sundress. His wife. All his. Though he was starting to think about sharing her with someone else....

As they finished up their well-earned

lunch, John suggested taking the long route back to the hotel to take in some more sights. With the sun high in the sky and the mercury edging up the thermometer, the summer dresses were out in droves exposing toned thighs and offering a tantalizing glimpse further up as the occasional summer breeze lifted up the flimsy cotton. John couldn't help but notice Liz's eyes being drawn to the same bronzed limbs and exposed breasts as his. Playfully slapping her tight ass, he leaned over to whisper in her ear.

"Anything catch your eye?"

She slapped his behind in response, pouting provocatively at him and raising her eyebrows before walking on down the cobbled street swinging her hips as she went. John felt his cock twitch in response as the possibilities started to work through his already ripe imagination.

Liz and John had often fantasized both about involving another woman in their sex life and about having other people watch them. The scenarios appealed to Liz's voyeuristic side and never failed to arouse her as John whispered in her ear. Tonight, more than ever, she was determined to feed the fantasy with a touch of something naughty. They'd fucked a lot since the wedding night. It had been romantic, intense, exciting, and drawn out. Now it was time for something wild and dirty.

Back at the hotel, it was time to freshen up and get ready for the night ahead. Their late lunch had served as an early dinner and so freed up their night for fun. Liz showered first and turned her attention to her clothes and make-up whilst John was in the bathroom. Flicking through the outfits in her wardrobe, Liz settled on a short, pleated skirt that she knew drove her husband nuts, and tight white t-shirt that clung to the curves of her bust and accentuated her perfectly flat stomach.

She dried her dried her stunning hair and applied product to help mold it into a tousled, just-out-of-bed style. Applying extra mascara, eyeliner and a coat of intense red lipstick, Liz looked in the mirror and smiled. She was fully armed to lead her hubby astray.

As he came out of the shower dressed only in a towel, commenting on how good the shower was, she knew when he stopped mid-sentence, drinking in the sight before him that she had hit the mark. She sashayed over to him, her hand reaching to feel the growing bulge under the small strip of material covering him, removing any sense of decency by gently rubbing her hand back and forth, squeezing until a quiet groan passed his lips, and his eyes closed, swaying slightly.

Her lips came close to his, brushing against them before moving to his ear whispering "not yet." He sighed in frustration grabbing for her, but she deftly leapt aside out of reach with a saucy grin, which only drove him crazier. Laughing he cast aside his towel letting the full effects of her teasing come into view, as always she was too quick, too nimble for him.

"Ok, ok, you win!" he relented. He moved to get his clothes from the back of the chair grinning to himself, firing off a parting shot. "You're going to pay for that later though!"

They went out into the evening, the setting sun casting its last rays over the tree-lined hills, which kept watch over the town, bathing the streets in a warm glow. The town seemed alive with possibilities to John. Every pert set of breasts straining against tight tops, every well-turned calf drawing the eye inevitably up the owner's thigh to the point where imagination takes over – John saw them all, watched to see which of them caught Liz' eye, which of them cast an admiring glance their way. It was when his eyes followed a particularly pert brunette around a corner that he spotted a neon sign that set his imagination going. Not exactly subtle, but a name that promised to deliver exactly what the night demanded: "Pussy Galore."

He didn't want to jump in too soon and

the night was still young, so he steered the apple of his eye into a bar across the road. Knowing the effect it inevitably had on Liz, he ordered another bottle of sparkling white and they hold themselves up in a dark, cozy booth near the back of the room.

They talked, laughed, flirted, and kissed. One of the things Liz loved about their relationship was the way that any night could feel like their first date. They genuinely never grew tired of each other's company, and the sexual chemistry certainly wasn't showing signs of dying out any time soon. She sipped on her second glass of the wine and contemplated the effect it was taking on her. Bubbles never failed to make her feel hedonistic, daring and, moreover, horny. She flashed a cheeky grin at her husband and brought up the moment back in their hotel room as they'd been getting ready.

"So, I take it from your hard-on earlier, that last night didn't wear you out?" She questioned.

"What do you think...?" Growled John in response. "Yesterday was just a warm up. I plan on getting pretty filthy tonight!"

"I noticed an interesting place across the road... might get us in the mood." Liz had the audacity to broach the subject but was tentative as she did so. She'd been admiring all the female forms out in their summer best throughout the day. She had visions of soft female curves and smooth, endless legs emblazoned on her mind. She wanted to switch these imaginary forms for a real visual. The strip club was bound to offer her just that, and rile John up no end to boot. She could picture the role-playing in bed afterwards. It was bound to provide the wild, uninhibited fuck they both seemed to be craving.

John couldn't believe his luck. The fact that Liz had brought the idea up saved him a lot of nervousness and uncertainty. His wife wanted to go and look at pussy – who was he to stand in her way?

"Really," he teased, "well if that's what you want, let's go for it."

The finished up their wine and made a move, slightly tipsy, across the street to the strip club. They paid their way in and headed to the bar to get some drinks before walking down onto the floor and selecting seats a few rows back. It was still early and they had the place pretty much to themselves except for a couple of groups of guys, both clearly on stag weekends.

It was a fairly low rent joint, as you'd expect for an establishment with such a name. The carpets were tatty and the lighting was dim, but as the curtains on the stage opened and revealed a Czech beauty dancing on the stage, it was clear to Liz that the décor didn't reflect the caliber of the girls. She grinned to herself as the tall, slim blonde moved effortlessly around the stage and the pole at the center of it. She felt her husband move his hand to her knee and start stroking it absent-mindedly.

"Perfect," she thought to herself, "he's clearly getting into it." She turned to her husband and quickly flashed him a grin, breaking their eye contact as the lithe stripper let her bra fall to the ground and revealed a pair of small, pert tits topped with impressive brown nipples. She was now cavorting in nothing but a pair of tiny briefs and Liz started to quiz John.

"What do you think of her? She's got a really nice tight ass!" She commented.

"It's her thighs," responded John, "just look at them. That pole obviously keeps her in good shape. Her body reminds me of yours, but your tits are bigger." Liz could see his point. The girl was tall, like her, and her legs were toned to within an inch of perfection. The muscles rippled smoothly and she hung upside down and stroked her hands down her body, drawing attention back to her natural breasts. The exhibitionist in Liz smiled at the thought of being in her place on the stage. How empowering it would be to have dozens of sets of male eyes on you, all clamoring for a wink or a sly touch.

'Pussy Galore' began to live up to its name, as the stripper relieved herself of the tiny panties she'd been wearing. She felt John's grip on her knee tighten as they got a view of shaved, Eastern European pussy gyrating on the stage before them.

"I bet she'd taste good." Liz whispered suggestively.

"Holy shit Liz, I love the way your mind works!"

The curtain closed on her act, and the two drank beers and compared notes on the stream of girls that followed her onto the stage. John was keen on the first girl, but Liz had felt herself drawn towards a smaller, petite girl. She was built on a tiny frame with very generous tits, shapely but firm legs and huge, innocent eyes peeking out from beneath her brunette fringe. Something about the sheer femininity of this girl peaked Liz's interest and John had noticed it.

The dancing girls were working the room between their turns on stage, talking and flirting with the clientele in the hope that they'd pay for private dances in the booths located at each side of the seating area. They were, unsurprisingly, steering clear of Liz and John. They were hardly likely to get private dances from a guy who had his wife in tow! This gave Liz and John the opportunity to whisper and giggle to each other about the thoughts the show was putting into their heads. John slid his hand a little further up Liz's leg and teased the top of her thigh under her tiny skirt.

"You'd like to get up there yourself, wouldn't you?" John queried. "Dancing around and showing off that perfect body of yours to everyone in here. I know you'd get off on it, knowing that these losers who can't get laid would be going home to jerk off over you!"

Liz had to admit he was right. The thought of other people finding her attractive really turned her on. She frequently fantasized about being caught naked, or even fucking John. The fantasies usually moved into the person catching them starting to masturbate in the corner of the room. She had shared some of these fantasies with her husband and they always got him going too.

"Mmmmmmmm, I sure would. Do you think these guys would like it?" On finishing her question, Liz turned towards John and ran her hands up her bare legs until she was pushing her already short skirt even further up, providing him with a quick glimpse of her black lacy thong underneath.

"How could they not, Liz? You're stunning and that naughty glint in your eye would drive them wild. You should go to one of those pole-dancing classes.

Imagine the fun we could have with what you learnt back at home!"

Liz giggled. What John didn't know was that she and Lisa had been going to those classes under the guise of Zumba for weeks before the wedding. She was planning a one-woman show for him upon their return back to their home in Bristol, but she was keeping that a secret.

Sipping on their beers and watching the spectacle before them, the newlyweds were feeling horny yet again, but Liz was adamant to get their money's worth before retiring back to the hotel room. She'd caught the eye of the petite girl a couple of times as she walked around the floor. She was wearing a tiny but tasteful dress, displaying the most incredible cleavage above its neckline. She seemed to be in less demand for lap dances than the traditionally Czech looking girls. Liz supposed it was because the guys here had all come to Prague for a reason, and this girl was exotic, sensual, but clearly not Czech. Or blonde.

Liz wanted more. She wanted a dance with that girl, while her husband looked on and built up a visual he could store for years to come. It clearly wasn't going to happen though, as the girls simply weren't approaching the couple. A nice thought though – she'd store it up and use it later.

"Another beer?" John asked her.

"Why not. I think I can manage for a bit longer, though you should be aware that I'll be keeping you up for hours tonight!" Liz declared bravely.

"I'd expect nothing else," replied John, "though now I'm going to have to wait a couple of minutes before I go and get those drinks." With that comment, Liz followed his glance down to his crotch and caught sight of the bulge that was growing. Liz's comment had clearly turned him on yet again. She loved the feeling of power it gave her.

She was left on her own for a while once John's erection had subsided enough for him to brave the bar. The young woman sat back in her chair and watched as a young lad was pulled from his seat and onto the stage by two feisty Czech strippers. He looked both mesmerized and terrified as they danced around him, grinding and teasing, while he remained tied to a chair in center stage. Liz got the impression he hadn't had much sexual experience and chuckled at the thought of him jerking off about this for years to come.

Her husband returned from the bar with two bottles of Staropramen and a huge grin on his face. Putting the beer down on the table in front of them, John beckoned to Liz to stand up.

"Come with me, I've bought you a

present."

Liz was both intrigued and confused as he led her away from their table. This soon subsided, however. John was walking in the direction of one of the private booths. They were having a dance!

John sat in a chair that had been placed in the corner of the booth and gestured at Liz to take her place in the main seat. At that moment, the girl she'd been watching walked in. Her body was even more perfect up close, and Liz swore that there was a wicked glint in those big green eyes.

"Hi Liz," purred the girl, "I'm Nina. Your husband tells me you liked what you saw?"

"Erm... yes, yes I did." Liz stuttered, completely amazed at what was happening.

"Well, in that case, sit back and enjoy the ride!" Nina smiled at this and pulled the tiny dress up over her head, revealing her fantastic tits spilling out of a black push-up bra.

Nina's back was facing John, and he caught Liz's eye deliberately, attracting her attention to the effect that the scenario was having on his eager dick. She didn't look for long though, as Nina was starting to move slowly around her, dancing and showing off every angle of her firm, curvy figure. She kept her eyes glued to Liz's and a hint of a smile on her face. The married woman was starting to think that Nina might genuinely be enjoying this. She pushed the thought to the back of her head. She was just a stripper after all, doing her job and looking forward to finishing for the night.

There was something very sensual about the girl. In every move she made, she portrayed herself as excited even turned on, rather than coming across as simply going through the motions. John was grinning away in the corner and his hand lay across his groin. Liz could just see his fingers moving very slightly. He was clearly aroused at the sight of his wife enjoying the attentions of another woman and was having to massage his cock gently through his trousers to cope.

Having demonstrated the full extent of her smoking hot form to Liz, Nina grinned saucily and lifted her leg. With one deft movement, she straddled the seated girl and proceeded with the lap dance. Liz's clit twinged and throbbed upon feeling the heat of the younger woman against her virtually bare legs. Her skirt had been pushed up still further by the stripper's bare thighs and their skin was in contact.

"I think your husband is enjoying this." Nina twinkled in her thick, husky accent.

"He's not the only one," whispered Liz. "You really are stunning. Thank you for agreeing to it. You know, with me being a woman and my husband being in here with us."

"No need to thank me. It's my job, but I enjoy it also. You are a very attractive woman. And you enjoy me, I can tell."

Liz couldn't deny that. Her thighs were trembling slightly with the excitement. She was grateful that she was sitting down and could therefore hide the damp patch forming in her panties. She and John may have shared their fantasy of bringing a woman into the bedroom vocally before now, but this was the closest she'd ever been to another woman. There was no doubt about the fact she'd be thanking her husband when they got back to the hotel!

It was at this moment that Nina unhooked her bra and unleashed her mighty cleavage. Her tits seemed to explode into Liz's face and she was enthralled by the sheer size and shape of them. Before she could stop herself, she'd let out a low moan. About to apologize for getting carried away, Liz was stopped from doing so as Nina whispered in her ear.

"The boys don't get to touch, but you can if you like."

Liz couldn't believe her luck. Her hands were pressed down by her sides and, without thinking, she opened up her rosebud lips to the nipple that was so close, and took it in her mouth. She was about to release it and apologize profusely when she felt something unbelievable. With nothing between their pussies but two thin pairs of lacy panties, there was no mistaking it. Nina was aroused and had released a flow of warm juice from her cunt that was soaking through her panties and onto Liz. Holy fuck!

Looking past this incredible, sexy woman, the newlywed saw her husband being less subtle now. He was obviously and unashamedly stroking his straining dick through his trousers and grinning like a man possessed. Liz couldn't wait to give him the relief he was so obviously seeking. She vowed that they'd leave straight after Nina finished her dance. There might be fresh beers waiting on the table back in the main hall, but they needed to get back to the hotel and fuck like never before. She felt wild and desperate for it.

Nina's eyes glinted at her again.

"There you go, I hope you enjoyed it. I know I certainly did. I'll leave you guys to straighten yourselves up. It's not busy so take the time you need. Hope to see you again soon." With a practiced ease, Nina had dressed herself as she spoke and shot a parting wink at Liz as she left the booth.

Liz was still sitting, dumbstruck, on the chair. Her skirt was pushed up around her waist and she was slightly concerned about revealing just how drenched her panties were.

"Babe – I need to take you back to the hotel NOW!" she commanded.

"No time for that, I'm afraid." Replied her husband. Liz felt disappointed. She'd explode if they stayed here much longer. But as John dropped his trousers, she realized that wasn't what he'd meant. He lifted her from the chair and turned her round so that her feet were on the floor and her hands were resting on the seat in front. Pulling her knickers to one side, he wasted no time in pushing his overexcited cock into her from behind and thrusting hard as he reached round to tease her clit.

She bit her lip to stop her from making any noise that would attract attention. She knew that with this kind of build-up, they could both come way before anyone disturbed them in the booth.

John's hand was rubbing frantically at her pussy now, in time with the deep thrusts from behind. Liz thought of what Nina would make of this, and conceded that she probably knew exactly what was going on in the booth. In fact, she was probably backstage fulfilling her own needs if the wetness in her knickers was anything to go by. These thoughts served sent a fresh wave of pleasure through her, and she whimpered to John as she began to come.

"Oh fuck. Oh, John. That's it, that's it..." She came, as quietly as she could manage, and prepared for John to do the same. Instead, he flipped her round and sat on the chair where she had been just minutes earlier with the stripper. With his cock in his own hand, he demanded his wife dance for him. She'd barely got his leg over his when he started to shoot hot, thick spurts of cum into his palm.

The next day brought more sightseeing and ambling around the city in the glorious weather. They'd been for lunch in the Old Town and then taken a leisurely walk down to the Charles Bridge. The couple had barely spoken about the events of the night-before, but exchanged the odd knowing glance and smile. They only had one night left in Prague, followed by a few in Venice. Then it would be time to head home and face the real world again.

A breeze was starting to pick up along the riverbank and Liz was ill equipped for the drop in temperature. John noticed her skin starting to pimple as her skirt whipped up, and suggested they head somewhere indoors for a drink. They'd come down to watch the sun setting but it was at least half an hour for doing so and he didn't want her catching a chill for the sake of it.

Liz agreed, and they walked arm in arm in search of a cozy restaurant where they could get an early evening snack and a beer. A comfortable silence lay between them and Liz glanced down at her wedding ring with a fond smile.

"Do you promise that we'll always have this much fun?" She asked her husband.

"I promise to do everything in my power to make sure that we do."

"I want to go back there tonight." Liz ventured. "What do you think?"

"I think that what my baby wants on her honeymoon, she should get." He grinned at the faux self-sacrifice. "We only live once after all, and it's our last night in Prague. I think Venice may be a little reserved in comparison!"

Once they'd made themselves at home in yet another dark corner of yet another Czech bar, Liz and John started to play one of their favorite games. It involved them pretending that they'd only recently met and the game was an intimate, two-person version of the student favorite "I have never." The premise was simple. One of them stated something that they'd never done, and the other one had to take a drink and then provide details if they had. Their version was fairly risqué and usually focused around sexual encounters. Far from being jealous, the couple both delighted in hearing stories relating to each other's sexual past.

They'd covered off the old favorites; Liz's fling with a minor celebrity when she was at University and the night John wanked five times after he'd been left high and dry in a nightclub by a mystery woman in the dark. She liked to tease him about that one – making out that she'd left a guy in exactly that situation and that in fact it had been her, years before they thought they'd first met. John knew this wasn't the case, as there was no way that he would have let Liz's perfect ass leave him alone in that room.

"I have never had a stripper cream her panties while giving me a private dance!" John challenged.

Liz burst out laughing, downed her drink, and then regaled the tale to John as if he'd never heard it before, let alone watched the whole thing less than 24 hours ago.

"Well, no wonder you want to go back," mocked John once she had finished, "sounds like you're onto a sure thing."

"My husband's definitely a sure thing. He's had a yoyo dick ever since we landed in Prague," laughed Liz, "I should introduce him to you, by the looks of things; you'd get along." With this, she looked pointedly down at the bulge in his pants and John grinned.

"What do you expect, after reliving that?"

They'd come to the bar earlier than planned and so there were still a couple of hours to kill before the club would open. The obvious solution was to drink lots more and continue with their game.

Liz realized that their plan meant not going back to the hotel to change. She excused herself to the bathroom to reapply her make-up and run a brush through her hair. Surveying herself, she was faced with a stark contrast to yesterday night's attire. Rather than the short slutty skirt and tight tee, she was wearing a floaty summer dress. She liked to think of it as demure but with a flirty twist. Unbeknown to her, John had caught people checking her out in it all day. The teal coloring was stunning against her auburn hair and green eyes. She decided that she'd do, and touched up her eyes and lips before heading back to join John at the table.

The night seemed to fly past and the drinks were going down just as quickly. Realizing the time, they finished up, paid the bill and made their way back to Pussy Galore.

It was quickly apparent that it was much busier than the night before and Liz wasn't sure if she was psyched or disappointed at the discovery. She may not get special treatment with so many willing young men, but then again there was more of a crowd to disappear into.

They found a spot and settled themselves down into it. Liz's eyes searched the crowd desperately, paying special attention to the girls that were milling around, touting for business. She couldn't see Nina anywhere, and her heart sunk. Still, they were in a strip club. They could sit back and enjoy the show, reflect on the night before and then go back to enjoy an after party for two. Simply being back in the club was sending a thrill through her again. She still couldn't quite believe the incident in the booth the night before.

John seemed to be reading her mind.

"Where's our hot little minx then? I thought she might give you a repeat performance!"

"Ah well – I guess she deserves a night off! Let's just enjoy the show."

A few girls came and went from the stage. Tonight's bunch were just as aesthetically pleasing as yesterday. Liz was looking them over appreciatively and imagining what it would be like to have their thighs wrapped around her while John looked on. Somehow she just couldn't imagine these austere beauties enjoying it as Nina had though.

They'd been there for an hour or so when the curtains closed on yet another leggy blonde stroking her pussy suggestively for the audience. Liz wondered whether they actually got anything out of it. If she were to stroke her pussy in front of an audience like that, she'd be horny as hell and desperate to come as soon as the curtains closed! She was roused from her thoughts, however, when the curtains opened again to reveal a small, dark-haired figure lying face down on the stage. Her round, firm ass was clearly accentuated by the silk French panties she wore and the cleavage spilling out of the front of her corset could only belong to one person.

As the music started and the girl rose deftly from her starting position, Liz's hopes became reality.

"It's Nina!" She whispered exultantly to her husband. "She's here after all – and looking better than ever!"

John grinned at her excitement and began to stroke her magnificent thighs under the light skirt of her dress. The skirt was much longer than the one she'd worn yesterday and so it was more obvious to any onlookers that he had hitched it up and was feeling the treats that lay beneath. But he didn't care. His wife was horny for a stripper and he was not going to kill her buzz!

He could see Liz's eyes alight with the possibilities flowing through her active imagination and moved his fingers slightly to softly stroke her clit through her panties. She shuddered and smiled at him. Man, he loved this woman!

Nina finished her act and the couple ordered more drinks. They were expecting her to do her rounds any time now, and hoped that she might stop by their table.

They were right, and she did start working the floor. She was in high demand tonight, however (after that act, neither Liz nor John were surprised!) and was being taken off to the booth by one man after another before she got anywhere near their table at the back of the room.

It had been a long night and they'd had far too much to drink. It was clear that no chance of any private time with Nina was going to materialize, so eventually the newlyweds conceded and began to get ready to leave. As John stood up to put on his jacket, a curvy, corset-clad figure appeared before them, an apologetic smile on her sultry face.

"Guys, hello again!" Purred the girl in her husky voice. "I am sorry I am not seeing you properly. Tonight we so busy. Full to the brim with drunks men! But I 'have a proposal for you. I finish in 1 hour only. I would like to come to your hotel with you and finish what we started yesterday. No charge. Just for fun!"

Liz couldn't believe what she was

hearing. She looked to John for approval but realized it was far from necessary. He was already nodding hastily in agreement and arranged to meet Nina out the back of the club in just over an hour.

John had spent most of that hour whispering in Liz's ear, sharing his fantasies, and enjoying his wife's form. He had teased her clit through her skirt, sat and watched an entire act with his hand gently caressing her pink, perky nipple and proposed that he simply sat back and watched later that night. He wanted to watch his wife with another woman.

The three of arrived back at the hotel in virtual silence. The tension in the air was unbelievable and Nina had been openly kissing and touching Liz in the taxi. Heading up to the room, John asked Nina if he should order drinks on room service.

"Not for me. I have little time. My boyfriend will expect me. I couldn't stop thinking about your lovely girl here all day. I need to enjoy her."

There was little that could be said to that, and they got into the room as quickly as they could.

Nina was certainly authoritative, part of the trade, Liz supposed. She held Liz up to the wall and kissed her again, harder this time, and pushed her breasts into her. Pulling away, she unbuttoned her long, woolen coat and revealed the outfit she'd been dancing in earlier that evening.

"Take off your dress now, Liz. You have seen me and now I would like to see you." Liz obeyed, and pulled the thin cotton number over her head. She'd not been wearing a bra and so was left standing in just her panties, being admired by both John and Nina.

"Oh yes. You are as beautiful as I thought. You felt me get wet yesterday, didn't you?"

Liz nodded affirmatively. She was lost for words as she and Nina started to writhe around the bed, feeling each other's warm, electrified bodies ready to burst. She had her mouth and her hands all over the huge, natural tits that mesmerized her as much today as they had done yesterday. Within seconds, Nina's fingers had found their way to her pussy and she cried out with excitement and delight when she found that this unusual English woman was already wet and ready for her.

As Nina's fingers teased and fingered at her tingling cunt, Liz was watching her husband. He was sitting on the chair, naked, with his cock in his hand. She knew he could come any second and reveled in that thought.

"Now we both lick," said Nina in her

slightly broken English. She moved herself round and positioned Liz in such a way that they could lap at each other's pussies. Wow – that felt good.

She'd never tasted another woman before and was surprised at how hot and sweet it was. Nina was completely shaved, and shuddered and moaned every time Liz moved her lips and tongue. The two of them were lost in a heady, intense place and before she could stop herself, Liz was shouting.

"Fuck, fuck. I'm going to fucking come!" All inhibitions and concerns had dissolved and she suddenly sucked hard on Nina's smooth, bald clit as she felt her own orgasm about to break.

"Oh baby, my baby, Jesus!" came John's voice from next to the bed. He was standing over them now, wanking furiously. His experience with women meant he could tell just how close the stripper and his wife were to coming and he wanted to join them.

"Oh Liz, your tongue is so good. You suck just like that, just like that. I come too," moaned Nina softly. As she finished her words, Liz felt the waves rising within her and began to cry out with pleasure like she never had before. Overwhelmed by the scene in front of him, John began coming before he realized that it was landing all over the stripper's huge tits. He was too horny to stop though, and he grinned in delight when he realized how much she was enjoying it. Her hips were bucking against his wife's mouth as she too succumbed to her climax.

The three of them smiled at each other, high on the adrenalin their orgasms had released.

"Is good to swing," Nina said, in a matter of a fact way, "I think you like. You should do more." With that, she dressed herself, kissed them goodbye and headed back out into the night. John and Liz looked at each other in disbelief, smiled, and began to kiss each other passionately. The memory of that night would fuel their fantasies for years to come....

4 UNEXPECTED EXPLORATION

Miranda didn't manage to utter more than two words to her mother, as they drove three hours from the house where she'd lived all her life to the halls of residence. At just 19, she was en route to start the next phase of her life. She'd been so excited, until now, studying to become a doctor as she'd always wanted. Her straight 'A' grades had afforded her a place at one of the best universities for medicine, and she couldn't wait to get her head back into the books. Only now, did it dawn on her how much of a change she was likely to be in for.

She had friends, the same ones, all the way through school, Jody and Luke. Like her, they were conscientious, quiet, and fairly shy. The three of them had fun. They went to the cinema, ate out now and again, and had plenty in common to talk about. They weren't the class oddballs, by any means, just not the life and soul of any party, and with no inclination to widen their social circle.

Now, the three of them were going to be miles apart, and Miranda was starting to wonder how she'd cope with such an alien world. She didn't really drink, with the exception of the odd glass of wine on special occasions, didn't go to parties, and had no clue, whatsoever, when it came to boys. She'd kissed Luke once, not because she liked him, but so that they could both get that awkward first one over and done with. Jody had kissed him for the same reasons, straight afterwards, so it clearly didn't mean anything.

The kiss hadn't been bad, though, it was hardly the experience she'd read about. All these books and films portrayed were weak-kneed, trembling moments that sent people into some sort of heady stupidity. The urge to tear off Luke's clothes and feel his hands over her body certainly hadn't taken over, and she could safely say the whole experience was mediocre.

So, what now? How would she cope with the giggling, drunk, party-girls comparing their sexual experiences? Miranda felt a flicker in her groin, at the thought. Though she had no experience of sex, she was aware of the effect that thinking about it had on her. The telltale tingle in her pussy and dampness in her panties had gradually increased over the last couple of years, and, eventually, she'd started to learn what to do about it. Since finishing her exams, the 18 year old had found herself home alone for long periods of time, while her parents were at work and her older brother was out with friends.

Taken over by curiosity during one of these times, she had locked herself in her bedroom (Miranda wasn't a girl to take risks, even if the house was empty) and began to experiment. She'd got off to a slow start. Gently exploring herself with her fingers felt good, and running her fingers over her clit sent shivers through her body. Her pussy was reacting and becoming wetter; its lips swelling tantalizingly. But it seemed to stop there. No climax seemed forthcoming, and she was clueless as to how to get there.

It was after several days of trying, growing increasingly horny and frustrated with each day that passed that she finally gave herself that joyful release. Applying a little more pressure with her hand and taking her time, she panted and flushed her way to that exhilarating first orgasm. Feeling a little dirty and ashamed afterwards, she showered and resigned to put all such thoughts behind her. It didn't last, obviously. She'd found her ticket to womanhood, and she started to make the most of it. So long as the secret was safe between her and the bedroom walls, she couldn't see any harm.

"Miranda," her Mother's voice lilted over the gentle hum of the engine, jolting the young girl from her happy recollections, "We're here. You were a million miles away sweetheart. What were you so deep in thought about?"

"Just nervous, mom. It's no big deal. I bet everyone feels the same way."

Safe in the knowledge that her secret was still just that, Miranda opened the car door and braced herself for the day ahead. It didn't take long to pick up the keys to her new room and lug the few boxes, and suitcase, into it. As a girl of plain and simple tastes, her wardrobe was far from what you'd call extensive, and it was the way she liked it.

The next couple of hours consisted of her mom fussing over everything and Miranda trying to shoo her out of the door. The other students that had arrived were all getting to know each other, and their parents had left hours ago. She was 19. Nobody knew her here. Maybe, this was her chance to meet new people after all.

Eventually, she was on her own. From

what she could gather, there were six rooms on the corridor, a couple of bathrooms, a large kitchen, and common area. It was a single-sex apartment, which was a relief. The thought of having to be comfortable around a bunch of guys was nerve-wracking. Steeling herself, she walked into the kitchen to meet everyone.

The kettle was on, and most of the girls were drinking coffee, chatting, and looking as nervous as she was. Miranda realized this with relief! Introductions were made, more nervous chatter ensued and, eventually, Helen, a confident, bubbly blonde, suggested opening a bottle of wine to lubricate the situation.

Helen looked the part. She was very slim and athletic looking, with long, toned legs protracting from her denim shorts. Miranda considered her own figure. She certainly wasn't tall, and she was conscious of her hips, which seemed to be a lot rounder than Helen's. Her breasts were fuller, too. Although she kept them well covered, she knew that was no bad thing. An hourglass figure, her mom always said. A plain face, framed by a mousy, brown fringe and glasses, was what Miranda felt really let her down. But what did it matter? She had brains, good grades, and a career ahead of her.

The wine was opened; Miranda accepted a small glass in a bid to fit in, and conversation turned to the courses they were enrolled for. Helen would also be studying medicine, Annie and Elise were to be science students, Rachel was a budding historian, and Eve had signed up for the Art History degree. Then, they talked about the people they'd left back at home.

From what she could gather, Helen and Eve, both, had hundreds of friends back home, including a few who were staying in different accommodations at their university, as well as boyfriends that they were going to try and maintain a long-distance relationship with. Elise had broken up with her boyfriend a couple of weeks ago, on the clichéd grounds that she "just wasn't that into" him, and Rachel hadn't yet decided whether it was boys, girls, or both, that really did it for her.

"Sex with Paul must be awesome, if you're willing to sacrifice all the hot new student talent for him!" Elise challenged Eve.

"Well, I definitely love him. We've been an item for nearly a year. But yeah, he's got a real knack for making me cum! In fact, he bought me a little going away present. Wait there..."

Miranda stared, shocked at Eve's confidence and brazen statement, as the freckly redhead dashed out of the kitchen.

Taking stock, again, she realized that more wine bottles had been opened, and she was the only one nursing the first glass. Feeling a warm, almost burning, sensation, as she gulped the rest of the liquid down, she reached out for the bottle and poured herself a refill. The teenager had never been around this sort of conversation. Though she had nothing to contribute to it, she hoped the wine may give her the confidence to ask questions.

"Here it is! How cool is he?" Eve looked triumphant, as she brandished one of the oddest-looking things Miranda had ever seen.

"A vibrator. He must want to keep you for himself." Helen chuckled, "Not that I blame him. So, is it a good one?"

Eve confessed to the other girls that she has yet to try it. "Paul saw me off yesterday, in more ways than one," she admitted, with a glint in her eye.

Miranda knew about vibrators, she'd just never seen one. She had also been under the impression that only porn stars used them. Now, she knew that wasn't the case, the shy girl was more curious than ever. Finishing her second glass of wine, she ventured the question, trying her best to sound cool and casual.

"So, how exactly did he do that?" Miranda could hardly believe the words had come out of her lips. Neither could the rest of the group. She'd hardly said five words in the last hour!

It turned out that Eve and Paul lived in a rural area. They had a secluded spot they liked to go to, drink a few beers, and just hang out. Yesterday had been beautiful, down in the South, so they'd taken a picnic down to the pretty place by the stream. Exactly where, it transpired, they had first kissed. They'd never taken it further than kissing and heavy petting there before. It was outdoors, after all, and they'd see the occasional dog walker, or farmer.

This time was different, though, and Miranda listened in awe, as Eve described how Paul had seduced her, so intensely that she no longer cared about being caught. He'd kissed her and gradually started stroking her perky, ample tits. Miranda couldn't help but notice them, braless, under Eve's thin shirt. He'd fondle them, until she could feel his horny, young man's cock trying to break free. Her clit was throbbing with excitement and, as she was wearing a dress, she simply pulled her panties to one side and invited him in. Paul had fucked her right there. Miranda was picturing a fit, toned 20-year-old guy with his top off and six pack rippling, as he thrust rhythmically in and out Eve's tight pussy.

Eve had not, yet, reached the point of

the story at which her intense climax had instantly triggered Paul to shoot his spunk deep inside her, when Miranda excused herself, suddenly.

"My mom," she cried, "I was supposed to call her an hour ago!"

Well, that was a lie! Miranda had got so hot and bothered, listening to Eve's al fresco tale that she just had to excuse herself to do something about it. Thankfully, her room was the furthest from the kitchen, where the noise was growing as the wine flowed more and more freely. She sank down, onto her new bed, and unzipped her jeans. Until now, she'd spent time teasing herself and gradually building up to cumming. Hearing others talking so graphically about sex for the first time had made her hornier than she'd ever been. She ran her fingers over the damp slit and rubbed quickly and frantically, amazing herself at the speed and intensity of the resulting orgasm. It was so quick that it was only after her climax that she became conscious of the fantasy that had taken her there – being screwed outside where anyone could walk past.

Brushing her hair quickly, and washing the telltale scent of herself from her hands, Miranda straightened out her clothes and returned to the party, in the kitchen.

Though she'd only been gone a few minutes, the number of people in the apartment had doubled. One of Helen's many acquaintances was a guy from her school who was staying in a nearby apartment block. He'd arrived with a crate of beers and four flat mates in tow, and the atmosphere was both livelier and more laid back than before.

Miranda would normally be nervous at this sort of gathering, but the wine had taken the edge off, and she felt emboldened by this new sense of anonymity. She didn't want to get drunk and make a fool of herself, but at least she could leave her shy, virginal persona back at school.

Grabbing a beer from the crate, Miranda scanned the room, for a cluster of people to join, and settled on Rachel's group. Other than Miranda herself, Rachel came across as the quietest of the group and had given very little information about herself. Her subtle outfit, soft features, and curly hair were comforting and made her seem approachable.

The lads were a loud and rowdy bunch, fuelled by the alcohol and the thrill of a whole new rabble of girls to try their luck with. Rachel was talking to a dark-haired, serious looking chap who came across as somewhat more reserved than the rest, and he welcomed Miranda nervously, as she went over to stand by them.

"This is Miranda," Rachel ventured. "She's studying medicine, too, so you'll have something in common." Miranda thawed, instantly, at the thought of finally being able to partake in a conversation she could knowledgably add to.

"Hi Miranda, I'm Ryan. It's nice to finally meet someone who's going to be studying as hard as I will! I was starting to think I was the only wannabe doctor in the first year!"

"Me too... I'm terrified about the first day of lectures, but I can't wait to get started either!"

The three of them chatted for a while. Then, Rachel meandered off, in search of another drink. Taking the cue to glance around the room, Ryan and Miranda's eyes simultaneously landed on the same scene. Elise was sitting on the sandy-haired guy's knee, kissing and laughing with him. Ryan raised his eyebrows.

"Looks as though Joe's made a good first impression!"

"Well, Elise made no secret of the fact that she broke up with her boyfriend so she could play the field here." laughed Miranda. "It looks as if she's getting off to a good start!" For the second time today, the words seemed to surprise the quiet, bookish girl, even as they fell from her mouth.

"She's certainly a pretty girl," Ryan commented, "but where's the fun if it's that easy? A guy wants a challenge, not a quick, dirty fling with anyone."

Miranda seriously doubted this, but didn't show it. Instead, she accepted the refill to her glass that was being offered and politely asked him about his girlfriend.

"Sore subject," he winced, "she dumped me a few weeks ago. I'm probably in the same boat as Elise's fella!"

"Oh, I'm sure that's not the case," Miranda attempted to sympathize, "maybe, she thought you'd like the freedom?"

"I'm not that bothered to be honest. We hadn't been together long, and I got the feeling that she wasn't that into me, anyway. Probably, just thought I was solid and reliable. People are always banging on about that. Solid and reliable is all very nice, but it gets you friends and nothing more. Nobody wants to sleep with solid and reliable, they just want to talk to you about the people they DO want to sleep with!" Ryan's hand flew to his mouth.

Miranda snickered, slightly disappointed at Ryan's indirect admission, but less than she made out to him. Excusing herself from his presence, Miranda walked over to Eve and Rachel, leaving Ryan looking at her peachy behind.

A few weeks had passed since that first night. Miranda saw Ryan every day at the university, and the two got on well. The atmosphere in the apartment was fun, but had sombered slightly since that first night, as the girls got to grips with lectures, essays, and reading lists. Helen had joined a couple of societies and was meeting loads of new people. Elise had lived up to her promise of playing the field. Her room was adjacent to Miranda's, and she'd seen a guy sloping off more than once.

Miranda had confessed her virginity to Rachel, and if she had been surprised, she didn't show it. Miranda suspected it was obvious to everyone who saw her. She pictured a huge sign floating above her head, declaring the fact to the world. For some reason, she had no idea why, she just couldn't bear the idea of Helen, Eve, and Ryan finding out. Anyway, for now, she had bigger things to worry about. They were having a party at the apartment tomorrow night, and Rachel had insisted the two of them go shopping for outfits. Miranda didn't really do shopping. She bought similar style jeans and sweaters, and that's about as far as it went. She was sure that wasn't going to be enough today.

Rachel greeted her at the mall, with a huge beam on her face and a credit card in her hand.

"Come on M, are you ready? It's about time you and I bought something wildly inappropriate, and took the limelight off those three vixens we live with!"

Thankfully, Miranda knew she was joking, and they made their way towards the shops. It wouldn't be so bad. She enjoyed Rachel's company, and besides, she liked the idea of looking good tomorrow and taking the others by surprise.

An hour later, she found herself cramped into a small cubicle with Rachel, at least a dozen dresses hanging between them. She was self-conscious, unused to stripping in front of anyone, even another girl.

Reaching for her first dress, Miranda turned to see Rachel standing before her, wearing nothing but a pair of black lacy panties. She fought to hide both her shock and arousal. Unlike Rachel, Miranda had no question marks over her sexuality, so the effect of seeing her firm, creamy C-cups was a complete surprise. Rachel wasn't skinny, but had a toned figure and soft curves. Her long, curly auburn hair framed her torso and perfect tits. A trimmed mound of hair was visible through the lace of her underwear and Miranda realized that she hadn't seen another woman's pussy before.

"You really are inexperienced, aren't you!" Rachel laughed. "Have you never seen another woman before? I'm pretty sure you're not into girls, so that doesn't account for the staring."

"Sorry..." Miranda stammered, "I wasn't staring..."

"Don't be silly. It's natural to be curious. Just as well it's me in here with you and not Helen. Here..." Rachel took Miranda's hand and guided it to her breast. "Touch it."

Gulping, Miranda slid her hand over Rachel's perky tit. They were smaller than her own, but completely different. She felt the small, pink nipple start to shrink and harden under her fingers. Emboldened, she moved her spare hand up, to feel both tits simultaneously. Squeezing them slightly, she allowed her thumbs to stroke Rachel's nipples for a moment, before removing her hands and smiling shyly.

"Nice boobs, wish mine were that pert!"

"Are you kidding? You've got amazing tits. I know you keep them permanently hidden, but I can't ignore those beauties all the time! Right, let's get you a dress that's going to really give Ryan a taste of what he's missing."

"What do you mean?" queried Miranda.

"I'm not trying to impress Ryan or anyone. You've surely just realized that I haven't got a clue when it comes to sex. I've only ever kissed my best friend, and I didn't even like him that way. It was awful!"

"You two have chemistry, you could tell, even on that first night. He certainly likes you and a bit of flirtation can't hurt. It's time for you to start realizing the power you have. Starting with a killer dress." The last comment came across as a command rather than a suggestion, so Miranda picked the dress that had been forgotten back up, and started to remove her clothing.

It was a fifties style, circle dress with wide shoulder straps and a high, square neckline. She'd chosen the style, because she knew the shape would flatter her curvy hourglass figure without being slutty, or low-cut.

"No." Rachel asserted firmly, "It's gorgeous, but too safe. You're going to a party, not a wedding! You need to give him a hint of something." She reached up, to the rail, for one of her own choices, a soft bias-cut number with a knee-length, floaty skirt and scooped neck, and handed it to Miranda. "Here, I won't take no for an answer!"

The girl took the dress from her bossy companion and removed all but her bra and panties before pulling it over her

100

head. Rachel whistled.

"Nice. Exactly the look you're after! Sexy, but not a slut or hooker in sight!"

"It's pretty low-cut," ventured Miranda, glancing down, at the cleavage that would be on display, where she not wearing a full cup bra that was protruding above the neckline of the dress. "I don't think I have underwear to go under it."

She was surprised, though. Looking in the mirror, she could see that it was pretty and sexy. The dress showed off her curves, while still being respectable. It was the color of a deep red wine and instantly portrayed her as a confident, experienced woman, rather than the nervous virgin who lived in shirts and jeans.

"We'll do something about that. It's underwear shopping time. You don't want a guy to get you to bed and discover one of those boulder-holders! You need a balconette. It will be perfect for that neckline and give you a nice boost. What's your size? Stay there. I'll go and get some for you to try."

"Erm, 32E," replied Miranda, looking nervous, again.

"Wow, lucky girl! Give me two minutes."

True to her word, the whirlwind was back in the changing room as quickly as she left. Triumphantly, she held a burgundy balconette bra in one hand and a matching pair of lacy French panties in the other.

"These will do the job perfectly." She was right. Doing a twirl in front of the mirror, Miranda beamed. Okay, it was a little more risqué than she was accustomed to, but this was a new start and a new image.

"Right, get 'em off! Let's get you to the register before you change your mind."

She pulled the dress off, much more comfortable at being semi-clad in front of Rachel, by now, and turned away from her to change her bra from the new to the old.

"No way," challenged Rachel, "you got to see me. Now, it's your turn. It might help loosen you up a bit."

Miranda conceded to the bisexual girl's request and unhooked the bra, letting it fall to the floor. She stood in front of Rachel, feeling very self-conscious yet a little empowered.

"Wow! They really are something else! Miranda, you have perfect tits and a killer body! I could tell you were hot under all those clothes, but I hadn't realized just how hot!"

It was Rachel's turn to look a little flustered, but rather than letting it bother her, she took a step towards the curvy girl in front of her and reached out to her bare breasts.

"Can I?" She questioned. "You touched mine. Now, it's only fair to swap!"

"Sure, it's only fair!"

Rachel reached out to Miranda's full, firm tits. Her beautiful nipples were already hard, and she couldn't resist running her hands down Miranda's sides, feeling the full effect of her killer curves. Both girls were aroused, but neither let on. Rachel had no doubt about what she wanted next. Miranda was wet. Wet and worried that if Rachel came much closer, she'd smell, or feel, her arousal through the skimpy underwear. Her clit twinged and throbbed when Rachel's hands ran down her sides.

One minute, she was trying to compose herself, the next, she felt Rachel step closer and slide one hand round her back, sending an intense shudder through her. Until now, she'd stifled a couple of sighs. This was impossible when Rachel boldly moved her hand down and ran her middle finger up the lacy fabric covering Miranda's pussy. Moaning aloud, there was no hiding how turned on she was, now. She knew Rachel could tell, but she no longer cared. She was hornier than she'd ever been.

Rather than being horrified at Rachel's actions, Miranda was praying that the other girl would continue the skilful work she'd started on her clit. The feeling of someone else's fingers probing at her pussy was overwhelming and so much better than it felt when she masturbated. She felt Rachel's breath on her cheek and her soft lips met her own.

Rachel continued to kiss her, gently but hungrily, occasionally, flicking her tongue in and out; it was nothing like the washing machine experience of kissing Luke. Although Rachel was still fully clothed, her white tee-shirt was thin and low-cut. Miranda stroked and squeezed those pert little tits she'd had her hands on earlier, and let out another low moan.

So intense was her excitement, she'd barely had a chance to think about the fact that they were pressed up against the wall of a tiny changing room. It was a weekday, and the shop had been fairly empty, but there was every chance they could be overheard, or even caught. They'd taken so many dresses in, however, she was sure the assistant would allow them a bit more time, before coming to enquire on their progress. Just thinking about it seemed to arouse her further, and Rachel's fingers responded, stroking her clit faster and harder. Miranda spread her legs a little further in response, and was delighted to feel Miranda slip a finger inside her panties and up into her soaking pussy.

"There you go, you like that, don't you?" Rachel whispered to her. "I knew you were highly-sexed, you just need liberating."

At this, Miranda had to reach her hands behind her to the wall for support. She was braced against the wall and her knees trembled, as she felt the combination of being fingered and having her clitoris stimulated, faster and faster, starting to build into an orgasm. Biting her lip, she felt pulse after pulse of the release soar through her body and smiled at the glint of satisfaction in Rachel's eye.

Well, she certainly hadn't expected that from the shopping trip! She felt a little awkward afterwards, but Rachel made her feel at ease.

"Don't worry," she assured Miranda, "I know you're not into girls. It was a hot moment, and I enjoyed every second of it, but look at it as exploration. Unexpected exploration, but exploration, nonetheless! There's nothing wrong with a bit of experimentation, and it'll help put you at ease when you end up there with a guy."

"I enjoyed it," admitted the more inexperienced girl. "It felt so much better than when I do it to myself!"

"Maybe, we should get you a vibrator as well, in that case. It's another feeling altogether. It won't beat the feel of someone else's mouth, or fingers, caressing your pussy, but they do give you a good, quick fix, if you get as horny as I'm starting to realize you do!"

CRBD

Running the brush through her hair one last time, Miranda surveyed herself in the mirror. She looked pretty good. Different. She knew that Helen and Ryan would be surprised at her new look. Cleavage on display wasn't her thing, but it made her feel sexy and a bit more confident. Or, was that just the memory of the last time she'd been wearing this dress in the changing room with Rachel the day before? A grin spread across her face at the thought. Applying some lip-gloss, she grinned at herself, in the mirror, and opened her bedroom door to join the rest of the girls, in the kitchen.

"Get you!" Helen exclaimed excitedly. "Looking hot with your baps out. Who would have thought it! Now, really push the boat out and have a glass of wine."

Rachel and Miranda exchanged a cheeky smile across the kitchen, and took glasses of cheap fizz from Helen.

"Let's have a toast. To cute boys and hook-ups for the singletons!"

They all laughed and drank to the toast. The guests wouldn't start to arrive for another half an hour or so, so they could relax and have some time to chat amongst themselves. Elise was regaling them with stories of her recent conquests and some of the wild sex she'd been having with one in particular. Only the day before, she'd been to a student night and been fucked by one of the DJs in the nightclub toilet. It brought a smile to Rachel's face, as she thought about her illicit encounter earlier that same day. An idea came to her then, and she wandered over to where Miranda was stocking some beers into the fridge, ready for the guests arriving. Pretending to help her, Rachel leaned down and muttered quietly to Miranda.

"Have you tried it yet?" She was talking about the small silver bullet-style vibrator that Miranda had picked out, after their encounter yesterday.

"Not yet," confessed Miranda. "I was nervous that I might be overheard. Plus, I don't really know what to do with it."

"Don't be dumb, your door is the furthest away. Come with me."

Rachel took Miranda's hand and headed out of the door, calling to the others to say she was going to try some make-up, in the shyer girl's room, before everyone else arrived.

She closed the bedroom door behind them and turned to face Miranda.

"I brought myself off twice, once we got home yesterday, and I'm still horny!" She confessed. "I thought we could kill two birds with one stone. Where's the vibrator?"

Miranda took it from her drawer and passed it to Rachel, confused and curious of what was to come. Rachel took it from her hand and laid, face up, on the bed, gesturing at Miranda to take a seat in the nearby chair.

Miranda looked on, with intrigue, as the other girl pulled her skirt up, her G-string down, and started massaging her clit with the vibrator. She smiled and moaned as it started to do its work, and Miranda was close enough to see Rachel's clit and labia start to swell with excitement. She turned the speed setting up, to maximum, and began to writhe around on the bed, her breathing and moaning becoming more rapid by the second, until her face suddenly contorted and relaxed into a smile.

Watching from the chair, she blinked with surprise. Rachel had just cum, pretty damn hard, by the look of it, in less than two minutes.

"And that," panted Rachel, "is why these things can be handy to have on hand. Watching you in that dress would have driven me wild tonight. Now, I've got it out of my system and you know how to use the bullet. Now, put some more mascara on, so it looks like we've actually been doing our make-up and go get Ryan!"

"I'm not after Ryan!" Miranda protested, not for the first time. But even, she wasn't sure any more. The incident at the apartment all those weeks ago didn't seem such a big deal, now. After all, she'd been getting her fixes, so surely, it was only natural that Ryan wanted the same.

Rachel straightened up her dress, put the vibrator away, and led Miranda back to the kitchen, where they topped up their glasses and joined in with the speculation about how many people would turn up, to the party.

A lot, was the answer. The apartment seemed to be bursting at the seams with young students, laughing and drinking. Miranda had locked her bedroom door, on account of the number of couples getting jiggy in the corners of the main room. She didn't want to find anyone at it on her bed!

She was a little deflated that Ryan, Joe, and the rest of the guys from that first night hadn't yet made an appearance. Still, she told herself, there's plenty of fish in the sea and she hadn't dressed up for him. Had she? Rachel kept sending cheeky winks her way, but Miranda didn't think for a second it meant anything. Her experiences with Rachel had been hot, horny, and very educational, but she wasn't a lesbian, that she knew.

Drinks had been flowing that night, and she was feeling very merry, despite her tolerance having increased a little during the weeks she'd been at the university. With a confidence she'd never dreamed of having before, she walked over, to a group of three guys, and introduced herself.

They were friendly and talked and laughed with her, sneakily checking out her impressive rack in the low-cut dress, whenever they could. It was at one such moment that Ryan walked in with his friends and clocked her, immediately.

"Jesus," he thought to himself. "What the hell happened to her?" Unsure whether to be excited, or concerned, at the prospect of quiet, shy Miranda with a killer cleavage and a group of guys vying for her attention, he made his way to the beer crates and helped himself to a can, before going over to join them.

"Ryan! You made it!" Miranda exclaimed. "This is Jamie, Rob, and Jack. They're all first years, too."

Ryan shook their hands and turned to the butterfly that seemed to have emerged all of a sudden.

"M, you look beautiful," he said, "... and confident. There's something different about you, but I can't put my finger on it."

"I think I'm drunk, that must be it," she laughed. "How have you found classes this week?"

With the conversation steered to safer territory, the two classmates chatted about medicine for a while. She started to notice how friendly and big his eyes were, framed by dark, sexy lashes. He, obviously, kept in shape and, while he was no Adonis when compared with the men

Elise brought home, there was no denying that he was attractive.

She thought she caught him sneaking a glance at her chest, a couple of times, but couldn't be sure. She was fascinated by the idea of flirting with him, but didn't really know where to begin and just wasn't sure she had it in her. Then, her mind flashed back to earlier in the evening, when she'd watched Rachel using the vibrator on her bed, and realized how ridiculous she was being.

"So," she began, "have you found a replacement for Miss Solid and Reliable, yet?"

"Ha, no!" Replied Ryan. "I've vowed to keep away from any women who don't actually find me attractive. More trouble than it's worth, otherwise. I've only met one worthy candidate, since I've been here and I'm not sure I stand a chance, anyway."

Miranda had been spurred on by the first part of his dialogue, but her heart dropped at the last sentence. "Damn."

"Still," continued Ryan. "Let's have another drink, or have you had too much already?"

They headed over, to the bar area together and vowed to get drunk.

Half an hour later, Miranda was feeling a little woozy, and it hadn't escaped Ryan's attention. She wasn't completely hammered, but she did need some water and to take it easy. He approached her and she agreed, saying she was going to lie down for a few minutes and could he bring a glass of water to her room.

Ever the gentleman, Ryan did as he was ordered and tapped gently on the wooden door, water in hand.

"Come in," called Miranda. "I'm just lying down."

Ryan offered her the water and demanded she ate the snacks he'd brought her, from the buffet. She started to feel a bit more human at that point, realizing she'd barely eaten all day in the excitement of the preparations.

"I'm so sorry," Miranda apologized. "I can't take my drink. What a loser!"

"Don't be ridiculous, Miranda, you're just a bit tipsy. You're obviously not used to the feeling, that's all. Here, can I sit down?"

Scooching her feet, she patted the bed, next to her, and smiled.

"Oooh, a man in my bedroom. Whatever will the others be saying?"

"Don't be dumb. They know you're not like that. Besides, they've probably not even noticed we're gone. Everyone seemed pretty preoccupied with having a good time."

At that, Miranda found herself encouraged and spurred on by her recent experiences with Rachel.

"Maybe I can be like that, when the situation's right..." Fixing her eyes on his, as suggestively as her statement, she trailed off. Ryan's inviting eyes widened, and he drank in the sight of her, before leaning in and stealing the first kiss.

The first touch of their lips was nothing short of electric, and they stayed there for several minutes, sliding, moving, changing their positions, and gently making contact with their tongues.

Glancing down, every now and then, Miranda was conscious of her figure, packaged perfectly in the neat dress. She was a woman. There was a man in her room. One that seemed to be very interested in what was underneath the frock, she realized, as Ryan tentatively ran his hand down her side.

Opening her eyes, Miranda took his hands and laid one on her knee and guided the other to her breasts. A look of understanding passed between them, and Ryan didn't need to be told twice. He stroked her knee and up, to her thigh, under the thin fabric of her skirt, as he absorbed the mighty cleavage that lay before him.

"Seriously M, has anyone ever told you that your tits are perfect?" Ryan uttered in wonder.

"Only once, and it was a girl," laughed

Miranda, aware that he would have no idea what she meant by that.

She was torn then. Did she confess her virginity, or just go ahead and hope? She decided upon the latter. She was horny again, and didn't want to risk him getting scared and pulling away.

She kissed him harder and deeper than before. He felt her sense of urgency and the force of her lust, and realized this was something new for him. This girl was actually attracted to him. She wasn't settling, she wanted him. Really wanted him, judging by the way she was pushing up against him, as they kissed. His already hard cock sprang and twitched a little more in his pants, and he silently thanked the universe for this moment.

Ryan had been fairly sure that Miranda was sexually inexperienced, but the way her hands ran over his torso told a different story. She was stroking and grabbing, in time, with their now frantic kissing. His erection was starting to throb and become desperate, to be freed from its confines.

Unable to wait much longer, he moved his lips down to Miranda's neck, and began teasing and kissing it gently. It was a sensation unlike any she'd experienced, and one which titillated her, more than ever. Pulling away from him, she stood up and lifted her dress above her head, and off.

She could see, from Ryan's face, that he'd no idea exactly what she'd been hiding under those baggy clothes, until tonight. Her 19-year-old breasts bulged out of the sexy balconette bra that Rachel had insisted she purchase and her ass was more pert and round in the French panties than he could possibly have dreamed. In between, her waist nipped in and her legs, while not long, were as curvy and firm as her torso.

Watching his reaction was empowering. He wanted her, and she was going to have him. She'd waited her whole life to see that look of desire, and now, she'd had it twice in as many days. Still standing before him, she decided to tease him a little.

Miranda ran her hands down her body, from the firm bulging tits down, to her lacy panties, where it hovered for a few seconds. Keeping an eye on his reaction, she summoned up some courage and eased her fingers down, under the elastic of her panties and started to massage her clitoris, right in front of him.

Unable to cope for much longer, the horny youth reached down and started to unbutton his jeans.

"Ah ah ah, not yet," declared the newly confident Miranda. "You can watch, but not touch."

Gob smacked at her sudden assertion, Ryan sat back down and watched the show. Both hands had moved to her tits, now, and she was massaging them seductively, right before him. Smiling coyly, she reached behind her back, unhooked her bra, and let it fall to the floor, exposing her erect, pink nipples and sending yet another twitch through Ryan's cock.

Torn between pulling her down, onto the bed, and continuing to watch where her current exhibitionism would lead, Ryan squirmed again, and smiled, laying his hand in his crotch, to provide some minor relief to his throbbing member. He thought about the shy girl he'd first met, only a few weeks ago, and how the lads had teased him for spending most of that evening talking to her, when there were so many 'easy lays' in the same room. If only they could see her, now! But this was his secret.

Miranda was feeling bolder and more empowered, by the minute. She had a captive audience of one and wanted to build him up, as much as possible, but was also conscious that the juices from her excited pussy were starting to run down her thigh. She craved his touch.

"You can strip, now, but stay there," she ordered, "I have one more surprise for you."

Ryan didn't need to be told twice and was sitting naked, on her bed, within seconds. Meanwhile, Miranda was reaching down, into her drawer. She took something from it. Then, she sat in the chair that was facing the bed and removed her soaking panties.

Catching his eye, seductively, she then switched on the silver vibrator, and started to really put on a show for Ryan, just as Rachel had done for her earlier. She moved the bullet slowly round her clit, and the boy's eyes bulged, as she spread her legs and showed him just how wet her neat little slit really was.

She kept the speed low, pulsing it every so often, for a second or two. She didn't want to cum, but it felt so good. She noticed Ryan's hand stroking, absently, at his cock. He was stopping himself from going all out and jerking off right in front of her. He wanted to enjoy cumming inside her and, if he did, it would be over in seconds. But his balls were aching and he could ignore it no longer. It was Ryan's turn to take charge.

"Bed. Now!"

Miranda conceded to his wishes, more through her own desperation and desire than anything else. She was simultaneously nervous and thrilled, at the thought of feeling cock inside her for the first time.

Lying on top of the sheets, Ryan began to kiss her neck, again, and moved down to the fine titties he'd become so fixated with. He took each nipple in his mouth, in turn, and sucked, until Miranda uttered a low moan. Meanwhile, his fingers were probing, slowly, at her drenched slit. He knew he could slide right in, if he wanted to and, wow, did he ever! He reached into his pocket for a condom and slipped it on.

"Right, missy, do you think we should do something about this?" He reached down and stroked his throbbing cock, right in her face.

"Yes, yes," she uttered, "but let me touch it first."

She moved her hand out and grabbed him.

"Oh, God Miranda!" Ryan cried out. "Fuck me, that's good. I need to take you, now, so badly, it hurts."

He wanted to taste her pussy with his tongue, but that was going to have to wait until later. Right now, he simply needed to enter her soaking pussy and screw her, which is just what he did.

Miranda cried out, as she felt a hard, thick cock push into her for the first time. So, this was what she'd been missing! She instinctively pushed her hips up, to take him deeper, and felt his pelvis graze her clit. Now, his cock touching something inside her that felt amazing.

"Holy shit, Ryan, that feels unbelievable."

"Tell me about it," responded Ryan, as he felt the tightest of pussy lips gripping him, even harder. "You're seriously hot, I can't believe this is the quiet, shy Miranda, with her legs wrapped round me!"

With that, he started to slide in and out of her with increasing pressure and speed. He knew he was going to cum quickly. There was very little he could do about it. It seemed he wasn't the only one, though. Miranda was breathing harder and harder, and emitting a little cry with each thrust.

"Oh fuck, yeah! Are you going to cum you sexy little minx?" Ryan cried.

"Yes, yes! Oh fuck YES!" Came Miranda's response. The contractions of Miranda's cunt around his cock, as she came sent him over the edge, and before he could stop himself, Ryan was shooting his spunk in the most intense climax he'd ever experienced. They lay there, sweaty and breathing deeply.

"Well, I had you down as a virgin when I met you," confessed the gratified adolescent, "but I see I was wrong!"

"No, you weren't," Miranda admitted, "that was the first time I've been with a guy. And, wow! What have I been missing!"

"You're kidding! I can't believe that was

your first time. It was incredible! And, completely unexpected!"

"It's all exploration," mused Miranda, "unexpected exploration."

With that comment, she smiled to herself, kissed Ryan, and looked forward to round two.

5 SPINNER'S SALOON

Bailey Kellman wasn't the typical dance hall whore. The buxom beauty with flaming red hair and emerald eyes played the part of one because it provided her the means to get what she wanted. And what Bailey wanted was a man – one man in particular.

Nothing good could be said about Caleb Winters. He was handsome enough – long, lean, with a wicked smile that could stop a runaway train dead in its tracks. She'd seen him flash that smile at the other girls, and every one of them had all but melted into a puddle at his feet. But it would take more than a pretty smile to knock her off track. She was a woman on a mission and that mission was him. Caleb Winters had met his match. He just didn't know it yet.

Circling the smoke-filled room, she kept one eye on Caleb as she made her way to the bar. He'd been sitting at that same poker table for almost 6 hours straight now, and she figured he was due for a break. Bailey turned and leaned on the bar and gave the short, squatty man behind it her best smile. "Walter, a bottle of Spinner's best, if you please. I got a customer that's asking for it."

Walter slapped his towel on the bar and speared Bailey with a look. Two-bit whores were a dime a dozen, and he ought to know as he'd seen his share come and go in the twenty odd years he'd tended the bar. But there was something about Miss high and mighty Bailey Kellman that set his neck hairs straight up. "Now, Bailey, you know the rules. Mr. Spinner saves the good stuff for his best customers."

"You see that cowboy in black at the table with Billy and Jedidiah?" Bailey nodded in the general direction of a table where four men sat playing cards. "He's the one that wants it. If you won't give the bottle to me, maybe you should take it over there yourself."

Finding which cowboy Bailey referred to was easy enough. Walter had noticed him the instant he had stepped through those swinging doors. A man like that dominated a room simply by being in it.

And though he had pulled his hat low to cover most of his face, Walter knew who he was. A hired gun who'd shoot first and ask questions later.

Letting out a disgruntle sigh, Walter pulled a key chain from his waist pocket and went into the back room. He returned seconds later carrying a bottle of Spinner's best. He gave the bottle to Bailey and for one split second, thought maybe he should give her a warning about her "customer." But just as quickly as the thought entered his head, it was gone. It was time Miss high and mighty got knocked down a peg or two, and that cowboy was just the man to do it.

With the bottle of whiskey in hand, Bailey sauntered over to Caleb's table and nonchalantly draped the bottle over his shoulder, using her other hand to rub his neck and shoulders. "Mister," she whispered softly in his ear, "You've been sitting here for quite a spell. Maybe you need something other than those cards to wrap your hands around."

Every hand at the table went dead still. Bailey watched in silent amusement as three pairs of eyes looked at her in amazement and...fear. Billy boy about near wet his britches and she could see him eyeing her and the tall, cool cowboy in black; his thoughts so transparent on his face that it took all her willpower not to laugh. Jedidiah and the prospector simply starred at her like she'd grown another head. The grizzly ol' bear of a man lifted a hand to scratch his long, gnarly beard, all the while his gaze flickering back 'n forth from her to the cowboy in black.

Several long seconds passed before Caleb raised his head and taking the bottle she offered, threw his cards on the table. "Deal me out fella's," he said, his voice deep and smooth. He moved to get up, scrapping his chair along the wood floor, and the three men at the table scattered like flies, grabbing their chips and mugs of beer. Caleb watched them make a hurried exit and then reached around, grabbed Bailey by the waist, and swung her into his lap.

"Well, hello there cowboy." Laughing, Bailey took off his black Stetson and placed it upon her head. She ran her long fingers through his thick mane of dark hair, skimming her nails against his scalp, down to his neck, and then drew him to her for a heated kiss.

His lips were like liquid gold and Bailey's only thought was that the stories of his kisses were not exaggerated. Their tongues danced, their breath mingled, and their skin heated. He moved his hands to cup her breasts, and as he toyed with her nipples, Bailey lost all sense of what she was doing – and why – and simply let his lips and hands work their magic on her. It was only when she felt him grow hard beneath her that reality kicked in and she ended the kiss.

Wow, was all she could think of, and as she cleared the cobwebs from her brain, she told herself to focus. She had a job to do and it wouldn't do to get all emotional about it. But oh, the man could kiss. Focus, she screamed to her libido. Focus.

Bailey smiled and ran a fingernail down a thin scar on his left cheek. "Woo there cowboy." She gave his lap a little wiggle. "We got everyone looking at us. And though I don't mind giving those wranglers a free peak...," she leaned in to give his lips a quick nibble, "I'd rather keep this a private party."

Caleb's blue eyes were stone-cold sober as he raked them over her, and then he smiled that wicked smile of his and Bailey felt her heart lurch. Focus, she repeated silently. Focus. She stood, and taking his hand said, "Don't forget the bottle, sugar."

He picked up the bottle and Bailey lead him across the saloon, up the stairs, and into a room down the hall. She didn't even have a chance to close the door before he turned, pushed her up against the wall and began a full assault on her senses. His lips closed over hers and he plunged his hot wet tongue into her mouth. His hands worked quickly, shredding her frilly green dress to pieces until she stood there in only her red and black corset and stockings. Once he had her out of the dress, he spun her around and pushed her roughly back up against the wall.

While his hands untied her stays, his warm mouth moved along her bare shoulder, leaving little patches of heat in its path. Bailey's stomach muscles knotted into a ball of molten lust. Caleb tossed her corset across the room and put his hands on her tits, rubbing them, flicking the pointy peaks with his thumb and finger. She began to quiver, to moan, and to move beneath his hands. When he finally allowed her to turn around, to touch him like he was touching her, Bailey thought to hell with focusing and gave in to the molten need burning inside of her.

She had him out of his shirt and vest within seconds. Running her hands down his muscled torso, through his dark, springy chest hair, she kissed him long and deep as her hands undid his belt buckle. But when those hands touched the cool steel of the six-shooters he had strapped to his hips, she got a jolt of reality and stepped back. Caleb merely laughed and picking her up, threw her on the bed.

Bailey watched him remove his holster and hang it on the bedpost. She continued watching as he unbuttoned his pants and stepped out them. And she couldn't help but emit a sigh of approval upon seeing his eight-inch cock standing tall and proud. She started to reach for it, but Caleb put a hand on her shoulder, holding her back. He took hold of his cock, began stroking himself until a small ball of pre-cum formed on the head. Then he grabbed hold of Bailey's head and rubbed his cock against her lips, her cheeks, before guiding it into her willing mouth.

Taking all she could handle, Bailey ran her tongue along the hard length of him. She cupped his balls with one hand, kneading them, and then used her mouth and tongue on them before returning to suck hungrily on his rigid shaft. Caleb began to rock gently, slowly, allowing her to set the pace. Running his hands through her silky waves of red curls, he urged her on.

"That's it, baby. Come on and suck me dry. Ah, yes..." Caleb said his voice husky with arousal.

Bailey's body tingled deliciously as she quickened her pace, her hand jacking him off as she ran her tongue over the head of his cock. Then in a flash, Caleb had her lying on the bed. Spooning, he made love to her flesh, his touch shooting off tiny sparks of need from her neck to her toes. She felt her woman juices flow and rubbed her ass against his hard shaft as his hand squeezed her breast.

His warm hand moved from her breast, down her flat belly, then down to her hot, wet pussy. Inserting one long finger inside her, Caleb used his thumb to tease her clit. Moaning, she began to rock against his hand. He nibbled on her ear and her neck, then shifting, lifted her leg and entered her from behind. She put her right hand on the headboard, reached around to grab Caleb's firm ass with her left, as he grabbed hold of her hips and fucked her hard and fast.

Every fiber of her being throbbed as his steel rod rubbed against her g-spot. And when Caleb used his fingers to tease and torment her clit, stroking it, grinding her tender nub beneath his hand, Bailey felt the orgasm rip through her, sending her over the edge.

But Caleb wasn't done with her yet.

Limber and agile, he moved above her and spreading her hips wide, thrust his swollen cock inside her. For a moment neither moved as their eyes locked, held. Then Bailey brought his lips to hers. The kiss was tender, gentle. She ran her hands through his hair, down his back, and digging her nails into his ass, invited him to go deeper. Slowly, she rocked back and forth, her butt sliding on the damp, cotton sheets.

Her woman juices flowing; Bailey felt

the hunger build again, pulling at her, gnawing at her. And when Caleb matched her stride for stride, she wrapped her legs around him, needing him to go deeper, wanting him to go faster. Faster, and faster, he pounded himself into her. Then with one final hard thrust, he emptied himself and Bailey felt his warm seed merge with hers as she exploded into a kaleidoscope of pleasure.

Minutes later, with Caleb snoring softly in her ear and his body wrapped around hers, Bailey told herself to get up and get the hell out of there. To simply go quietly in the night would be the best – and the easiest – thing for her to do. But knowing that only complicated matters more. She'd taken an oath. And though she wasn't a coward, she was very much afraid that she was going to violate that oath.

Shifting slowly so as to not wake the sleeping man beside her, Bailey studied Caleb's face. His features were relaxed in sleep, and now would be the perfect time to carry out her mission. It was how she had planned it after all – to get him alone, seduce him, and when he slept, to tie him up and drag him back to El Calina. Easy enough when she had first visualized it but nothing about it was easy now.

She ran her fingers lightly along his cheek, felt the stubble of his beard as she traced his jawline from ear to chin. Need began to dig its claws into her once again and made Bailey pull her fingers back. Taking a deep breath, she willed her beating heart to be still. Yet even as her heartbeat slowed, she felt the warmth of his fingers on her breasts, drawing lazy circles around her nipples. Bailey's heart stumbled, thumped hard against her chest.

Giving into the need, Bailey turned to Caleb and kissed him hard on the mouth. She raked her tongue along his teeth and moving her hands down the length of him, found his shaft rock hard. Stroking, her hand gliding over him, she deepened the kiss until he shifted and trailed his lips down to her tits. They were enough to fill a man's hand, and as he feasted on them, the needy ball of lust simmered, sparkled, setting her on fire.

Moving above her, down her, Caleb took hold of her butt and lifting her, darted his tongue into her hot, wet pussy. Bailey's body bowed under the onslaught. He nipped, suckled, and gnawed on the engorged nub, his tongue lapping up her nectar. And as Bailey's senses shattered, he reared up and buried himself deep within her.

Bodies slapping and hearts pounding as

their moans of passion echoed in the dimly lit room; they flew up the treacherous cliff. And as her orgasm imploded in the center of her and reverberated all the way to her toes, Caleb kissed her hard. Then both of them tumbled over the cliff and into oblivion.

Sunlight slithered through the thin curtains hanging on the only window in the small room. Bailey laid there, her body aching and her heart cracking. She heard Caleb's snoring, felt his hard body behind hers, and this time when she told herself to get up, she did. Retrieving the chamber pot from under the bed, she relieved herself and then went over to the wardrobe. Buried beneath several layers of undergarments were her saddlebags and the only set of clothes she could call her own. Pulling them out, Bailey dressed quickly. The mud-colored pants and shirt didn't flatter her, but Bailey didn't care about fashion. They were comfortable and that was that mattered.

Picking up her boots, she walked as quietly as she could over to the only chair in the room and sitting, slipped them on. Silence hung like a thick cloud in the room, broken only by Caleb's snoring. And as Bailey ran her eyes up and down that gorgeous length of him, she shook her head and let out a heavy sigh.

No use telling herself to focus. The game was over and she'd lost. There's nothing to do but tuck tail and run. She could lie to herself and say another day, another time, but Bailey had learned the hard way that lying to yourself only caused more problems than it was worth. So, she got up from the chair and headed across the room. Pouring herself a shot of whiskey, she gulped it down and let the fiery liquid drown out the sour taste of failure.

Behind her, the bed squeaked, and Bailey's heart stopped. Oh shit, she thought, pouring herself another drink. As her mind raced to find something to say, Caleb reached around her and took the glass from her hands. His breath was warm on her cheek and she could all but feel the heat of his naked flesh through her shirt.

Once he had drunk the whiskey, he sat the glass on the table and trapping her against it, whispered softly in her ear. "Going somewhere?"

Words failed her. She couldn't think of one witty reply. And as Bailey splashed some more whiskey in the glass, she turned and locking her eyes on his blue ones, decided on the truth. "Home. I am going back home."

Caleb raised his brows. "Home? Now

why would a pretty lady like you want to go back home?" Leaning in, he tried to kiss her but Bailey put a hand on his chest and pushed him away. Confusion etched his face, then he smiled, and stepping back, gave her a mock bow. "Then by all means don't let me stop you."

She figured there would be time later to kick herself black and blue, so no use doing it now. Raising the glass to her lips she said, "Thanks for the ride cowboy."

Grabbing her hat and saddlebags, Bailey practically ran from the room. She needed to get as far away from him as she possibly could. She hurried down the stairs, into the backroom of the saloon, and out through the back door. Calling herself every low-life name she could think of, Bailey got her horse from the livery stable and saddling up, rode hard in the direction of El Calina.

Up in the tiny room above Spinner's saloon, Caleb picked up his pants and took out a folded sheet of paper from one of the pockets. He poured himself another whiskey, and with the paper in one hand, and whiskey in the other, he sat down on the bed. Unfolding the paper, Caleb read it as he sipped his drink.

It said, "Just wanted to let you know there's a bounty hunter on your trail. Ambush will take place at Spinner's saloon so best avoid that place as much as possible."

Folding the note, Caleb finished off his whiskey and smiled.

6 BREAK FREE

Savannah gave a final pat to her French braided hair to make sure that it was in place. She considered her hair to be one of her best assets as she was blessed with a long mane of thick, straight, and lustrous blonde hair that came up to the start of her hip curves. She had a delicious body with satiny smooth flowing skin and perfect curves at just the right places. It was an everyday routine for Savannah to do her hair after having her bath and before dressing up for work. She liked it that way. That way she got more time to do what she loved; and that was gazing at her naked body in the large mirror of her dresser. She knew that she was attractive. She wasn't misled by the misconception of being the most beautiful girl in the world. But she was certainly aware of the power she held over men; and she liked to reconfirm her power from time to time, as it was very important to her.

Savannah touched her boobs next. She always did that. Looked at them from every angle to admire and ascertain her perfection. She was proud of her breasts and liked to showcase them with as much elegance as could be imagined. Her impeccable dressing style added to the beauty of the vision that she cultivated. She smirked at herself with pride and dressed in a red-colored blouse with a black pencil skirt. She checked her phone and saw fifty-three missed calls and four messages. She was running late once again, which wasn't unusual for her. She was going to cover the Westfield mall protest live from the scene itself. She wasn't worried though because being the most watched reporter on the second best news channel in the state definitely had its own perks.

"I am here and I don't need a script. Let's just start rolling." She commanded as soon as she saw Dave, her cameraman.

She was expecting eagerness and hurry in Dave's actions, but all she was faced with was a blank look.

"Oh, so she doesn't know!"

The deep husky voice came somewhere from behind her. It was followed by a hoarse chuckle.

She turned behind to look at who it was and stopped short of falling right on her ass, and she was taken by surprise to find that the man was standing much nearer to her than she had expected. He was so close that she could feel his breath on her face. It smelled of mint and cigarettes, and something tickled at the bottom of her belly. She jerked back to get a grasp on herself.

"And may I ask who are you?" She managed to spit out the words with as much contempt as she could manage. She asked in spite of recognizing the voice right away. How could she not? He was her best and the only competition working on the rival news network that ranked at number one in the state.

"I am the one who is replacing you as the new live broadcast reporter, sweetheart. I hadn't imagined that I would have to give you the news myself though!" Another sneer followed the sentence.

She couldn't process anything for quite a while and kept staring at the long defined line of his handsome jaw. His steel grey eyes made her feel like he was looking at her absolutely naked and oddly, she liked it. She was taken aback by how much the little grey here and there in his thick black hair complimented the grey in his eyes. He was the kind who could wear any kind of clothes with equal charm. She had to stop that train of thought in order to regain composure. It wasn't like her to lose control like that. It was always she, who had an effect on people.

Joshua Baker, her archenemy, had somehow managed to land her job. He stood there grinning at her and with a look of amused observation on his face. Maybe she was giving away too much through her expressions. She cleared her throat and barked.

"Sadistic people like you may have to create illusions like these in order to satiate their hunger for success. But that's not me. So what are you doing here, Mr. Baker? Apart from obviously trying and failing at irritating me?"

If he wasn't amused then, he definitely was at that sally. The smile on his face grew longer as he looked at Dave and said, "She doesn't believe it, Dave! You were right; she is too self-absorbed to realize what is happening around her."

Savannah looked at Dave with her mouth gaping and eyes widening in disbelief, but before she could confront him, Joshua had a cell phone pressed against her ear. He said, "Talk to your assistant producer; her words will be authentic enough for you I am sure."

All that happened next was a flash for Savannah. All she could remember was being extremely pissed off and growing red in her face. Joshua was right indeed. She was replaced.

She woke up panting hard. Her heart was thudding away in double time, but it couldn't have beaten the throbs in her cunt. Her throat was parched but her forehead was gleaming with sweat. She couldn't believe what she had just dreamt. She was ashamed and she pushed herself back on her bed in frustration. How could she have imagined that? She could understand her sexual desires reflecting in her dreams, but she couldn't understand the need to be dominated; especially by her evil new colleague who didn't find anything good in her. In all her sexual relationships with men over all the years, she had gotten gentle love making. Every guy had treated her like a prize doll that would break if they were too rash, and she had liked to feel that way. It made her feel powerful over all the men. But she had just dreamt of being used like a slut by Josh.

She forced her eyes shut but couldn't rid the images that had set her heart racing. The vivid image of her bending straight from her waist and touching the floor while Josh fucked her sweet hole from behind didn't budge from in front of her eyes.

Her clit started swelling again.

She always slept naked in the bed, and she couldn't stop herself from touching her hard nipples protruding from her heaving chest. It sent waves of pleasure across her body right down to her curled toes. She grabbed each nipple between two fingers and pinched and pulled them. The pain gave her pleasure and a soft moan let out her lip. She couldn't bear anymore self-play, and she lowered her hands to her cunt, which had become a greasy hole by now. She immediately inserted one finger in her cunt without any difficulty. She was imagining it was Josh's finger. The second finger followed soon after. She was moving them in and out without any respect for her cunt. She wanted to be rash with it today. She folded both her legs at her knees and pulled them close to her chest. She wanted maximum penetration of her fingers because she was restless to find that spot that drove her into ecstasy.

Oh! How much she wanted Josh to fuck her like that. She wanted her legs to be rendered useless as Josh used her cunt for his own pleasure. She could imagine his steel grey eyes looking at her helplessness and laughing with pleasure. There was a third finger inside her now.

With her thumb she touched her clit, and that was enough to throw her into throes of pleasure. She was so close to cumming it was just a matter of a couple minutes. She rubbed her clitoris lightly in an effort to prolong her pleasure and postpone the waves of ecstasy by a little more time. She was enjoying it too much visualizing Josh biting at her nipples while growling with pleasure as he roughly moved in and out of her beneath.

But she just couldn't stop herself from spiraling down a very bright and endless ladder that landed her in a thud at its last step.

All that remained was her gaping mouth that was desperately sucking in air and the thumping heartbeat that reverberated in her ear drums loud enough to make her wince.

She pulled her hand off her cunt in an urgency that conveyed shame. Running into the bathroom, she started the shower and let it wash off her thoughts with her cum.

Pacing back and forth in her office wasn't helping Savannah in any way. She wasn't able to get rid of the unusual frown on her forehead and neither was she able to come up with enough courage to confront Joshua with her demand. Her assistant producer, Emily, had confirmed that Joshua would be replacing her on live broadcasts citing incomprehensible reasons such as the channel needed a new voice to deliver breaking news. After the meeting, Savannah had stormed in the office headquarters demanding explanations but to no avail. Apparently, the motion had already passed by her seniors, and all that she could now do in hope at having a chance of regaining her position was to patiently wait and do the other jobs that were presented to her. Hopefully, the new voice would turn old soon and she would be in demand again. Although she had given up on that, she definitely wasn't ready to give up on one honor, the biggest event of the year for any news network; the national award ceremony was coming up in the next week. Just one reporter from each network was to be honored by being present at the event, and most obviously it had been going to be Savannah from the network. At least until Mr. Joshua Baker had shown up. She had to confront Joshua with the demand that he allow her to attend, and so she stormed in his office without knocking.

"I have very important business to talk to you about, Mr. Baker, and you better take me seriously." The words flew off her tongue as she rushed in his office.

Joshua looked up at Savannah with no surprise whatsoever and blew a ring of smoke from his mouth. Savannah noticed the cigar in his hand. She looked back at him with a frown and immediately flushed as she remembered the disgraceful turn of events from that morning. She looked down at the carpet and with feigned anger spat out, "I have come to terms with you replacing me on the live broadcast, but I will not tolerate you crawling your way through to attend the biggest event of the year."

She looked up at him and saw the look of concentration on his face.

"I have been working my ass off for this honor, and I definitely deserve to go this year. So you may very well stop dreaming about it. For whatever reasons, you left your previous job and joined your rival company. I am sure those reasons will console you enough when you miss the event."

She tried to smirk at that but managed it very unconvincingly.

"Ms. Billmore, I am very sorry but I have already been asked for the honor, and I have confirmed my visit. However, I may change my decision if I am assured that you are desperate enough for this opportunity."

"I am willing to kill you to grab this

opportunity. Is that enough desperation for you?" Savannah barked.

Joshua had a hearty laugh and replied, "I like watching you squirm. You know, Ms. Billmore; I have always hated to watch you on television broadcast. You had an air of overconfidence in you. I don't like overconfident girls and I feel like fucking them out of their minds."

Savannah gasped at that. She couldn't think of a possible reply that would save her dignity. While she was still thinking, Joshua walked toward her. With one finger he traced the outline of her heart-shaped face starting from her forehead to her chin. The consequent raspy breath that left Savannah's mouth made him laugh with contempt.

"I like setting such girls straight. I like them to be shown their place. That's just my way of treating them. So Savannah, how bad do you want to go to this event?"

Savannah wanted nothing more than to storm out of his office but she couldn't move. It was as if she was under a spell and rendered out of control over her own limbs. She was surprisingly aroused by Joshua's words. She wanted him to fuck her so bad that she forgot to put her self-respect first. She wanted him to show her what she deserved. She wanted him to be her Daddy.

Suddenly, she felt wet lips on her own. Josh slowly engulfed her upper lip and sucked it, then her lower lip –almost as if he was checking them for their worthiness. He bit her lower lip so harshly that she screamed in pain. She could taste the rusty flavor of her own blood. She pushed him away in fear and anger.

She turned her back toward him but didn't rush out of his office. She couldn't bring herself to. Her tightened nipples didn't allow her to. She was trying to make sense of her feelings when suddenly she felt her hair being lifted from one side of her shoulder. She stalled in anticipation of a kiss on her neck as every cell in her body froze in place. All she got was a blow of air from Joshua's breath. It was better than a kiss. She was so turned on by the breath that she wanted to be naked that minute. That thought was followed with a piercing bite on her neck. She winced yet again. If she was to do this, she knew that it would be nowhere close to her usual type of sex. With all her usual men, she always knew what followed. But with Joshua she was betting herself for her pleasure. She was strangely thrilled by the idea. With some regained confidence, she turned back to look at him and said with a smile, "So you want to fuck me, huh? You want to show me my place? Are you sure you are up for it?"

In an unaccountable flash of a second, she felt something whip at her face. Joshua had slapped her.

She scowled at him while covering her cheek with one hand. Her breath came in rasps and she was finding it increasingly difficult to breathe, as each passing moment made her realize the gravity of her insult. She was too used to being worshipped by people for what she was. She was never insulted.

He saw the look on her face and came close. She stood stock still with the hand on her cheek, didn't move or budge as he was approaching. He was now close enough to breathe on her again. That warm fuzzy blow of air which made the hair on her neck stand and shiver.

He carefully used one finger to deftly pick up a fringe of her hair that had landed on her eye with the slap. He pushed it back and put it behind her ear.

Savannah stared at him with confusion. Nothing he did made any sense to her.

The other hand swiftly moved behind as it grabbed the small of her back and with a single strong move he pulled her toward him leaving no distance in between. Her breathing rate hiked and her chest swelled in her tight blouse moving up and down with each breath. His hand moved from her back to her hair as he grasped some hair at the nape of her neck and pulled gently.

"Why are you still here? What do you want from me? Tell me before Daddy slaps you again." He said hoarsely.

She could feel his hardness even through the thick material. She wanted to drop down that minute and free his member. But she couldn't. She had lost all control over herself and didn't react at all.

Joshua tightened the grip on her hair and pulled it. Savannah felt so much pain that her eyes became moist.

"Tell me you whore. Why are you still here? What do you want me to do to you?" Joshua spat.

"I...I...I want you to fuck me," Savannah managed to speak.

Joshua grabbed a breast cup of Savannah's blouse and squeezed it a bit too hard while still not loosening his grip on Savannah's hair.

"Why?" He demanded.

"Because I want to be reminded of my place," Savannah said with soft tears flowing down both her cheeks.

"If you want to be fucked, you have to let me fuck you the way I want to. And I will fuck you in all your holes." Joshua said.

Savannah's clit swelled hearing that. She could feel the flimsy material of her panty soaking in her own wetness. She simply nodded and Joshua released the grip over her hair and her breast.

He leaned back at the table front and said, "Strip for me."

Slowly and extremely self-consciously, Savannah shed layers of her clothes until she was completely bare. Her skin was radiant and although she looked beautiful, Savannah had never felt more ashamed and helpless before. She looked up at Joshua and said, "Please, fuck me!"

Joshua came close to her and holding her face in one hand, he kissed her. His tongue went down then scoured the depths of her mouth, and he sucked the air out of it. He pushed his tongue in and out and tongue-fucked her mouth. His other hand grabbed her boob and he was squeezing it with lust. It was difficult for Savannah to concentrate as she was exploited pleasurably. Suddenly Josh left her. He unbuckled his belt and threw it aside. Next, he unzipped his fly and to Savannah, that was the sound of freedom. She had never quite seen something like it. His cock was enormous. It was long and had the girth that almost frightened Savannah. She dropped down at her feet and grasped his dick hungrily in her hand. She wanted to taste it. She wanted his entire length to disappear inside of her. She licked the precum off his dick.

Just before she could suck down on his dick, Joshua pulled her hair again and said, "I am the one who is going to fuck you. Get up!"

He pulled her up by her hair and dragged her to a couch in his office. He threw her on it and she landed on her back. He climbed on top of her placing both his knees around her shoulders. His nuts were now near her chin as he was holding his dick and jerking it before placing it in her mouth. He could see scare in her eyes and it made him happy. He put the head of his cock in her mouth and said, "Suck me you bitch! Let me fuck your mouth."

With that, he began pumping his dick in her throat as both his hands grabbed the hand rest of the couch for support. He could hear Savannah gag underneath him and he laughed even harder. He had never seen something as beautiful as her face and he enjoyed it – that he had her all under his control. He could see her saliva mixed with his precum flow out of both the sides of her lips with every thrust as her mouth couldn't accommodate all of him.

Joshua removed his dick out of her mouth and bent to kiss her. He kissed her deeply then slowly and deeply, savoring every bit of her beauty and claiming his right upon it.

He then looked at her and saw a desperate want in her eyes. She wanted him to fuck her. Ms. Savannah Billmore, the lead broadcast reporter of the network, who could have any man she wanted at her feet, wanted him to fuck her brainless.

He lifted both her legs in his hand and bent them at her waist. He saw her cunt was overflowing with her lubrication. The pink of her cunt invited him inside and he placed the head of his cock on top of it pushing just a little inside. Savannah held her legs more toward her chest in anticipation of a deep fuck. But Joshua wanted to play. He didn't move in. Instead, he used his finger to draw down some lubrication from her cunt hole to her anal hole. He circled the tight hole and Savannah felt shivers in her spine. He pushed a finger in her anal hole with difficulty and saw Savannah gasp and writhe in pleasure.

Suddenly, he pushed in her cunt with his long and hard as stone dick all at once. Savannah screamed in pain and looked at him with eyes wide. He just smiled and sealed her lips so as to contain her noise within the office.

He pulled back extremely slowly creating anticipation and pushed in fast again. That made Savannah moan loudly in Joshua's mouth. Joshua was enjoying doing that to her. He touched one of her breasts and twisted her protruding nipple in two fingers pulling it toward him while continued to thrust in Savannah's cunt with slow defined moves that made her arch her back and moan with pleasure. He was aching to drink her breasts, and so he covered her mouth with his hand. He moved down to her breast and sucked on her nipple.

He bit it at first, then pulled and tugged at it. He saw Savannah close her eyes in pleasure when he rolled his tongue in circles over her nipple. He started going fast in her. He grabbed both her hand and pushed them above his head pinning her down and creating balance enough to move off his knees. He balanced that way on his elbows with his legs in a straight line and his hips moving forward and backward. Each thrust was delivered with eagerness, as Joshua wanted to fuck her deep.

Savannah was climbing on the tops of an unending mountain from where she was going to be thrown off head first. Josh moved one hand down to her sex, and with just one flick of her clitoris, Joshua saw Savannah twitch her cunt on his dick and spasm in a huge orgasm. He kept driving in her against the contracting force making her run out of her breath. With a deft move of his hand, he lifted Savannah from under him and made her sit on all fours on the cold marble floor. He sat behind her and slapped her ass. Savannah yelped with the cold bare flesh hit. Joshua started fingering Savannah's asshole using her own lubrication and increased the number of fingers one by one. Once he had opened her widely enough to push his cock in, he started penetrating her asshole.

Savannah cried in pain, as she had never been fucked in her ass before. No man had ever dared to ask her for that, and no man she had ever been with had enough courage to do it without asking. But there she was, on all fours bare on a cold floor, with a man who was using her body for his own pleasures. He was doing things to her that she had never imagined she would feel. He was entering unchartered territories that threw her in the realms of unadulterated pleasure, and though she was experiencing pain like never before, she never wanted it to end.

She wanted to be one with him through all her holes. She wanted him to keep fucking her like that.

Joshua made way for his cock in her ass, and once he was deep in, he grabbed her hips and started pumping relentlessly. He couldn't bear to tease her anymore as the tightness of her ass was making it difficult for him to control his orgasm. He drove into her as he grabbed her breasts from behind and dug his face in her back as he tried controlling the grunts that leapt out of his mouth in time with his thrusts.

Once again, he brought his hand to her front and found her clitoris. He flicked it with no mercy and soon she was in spasms beneath him. Seeing her in pleasure, he let himself flow with his impending orgasm.

As he drew himself out of her, she could feel drops of his cum trickling down her asshole and cheeks. She collapsed on the floor head first and he collapsed on her. Before Savannah could regain her breath, Josh was off her and had started dressing up.

"Sure you can go to the event; anyways I was never invited to go." He said with a smirk.

Savannah sat up and looked up at him in disbelief. Getting up, she dressed, and this time she did storm out of his office. She was furious but satisfied like never before. She could get back at him for his demeanor, but she could never regret letting him fuck her.

AUTHOR'S NOTE

Readers: I want to expand a few of the stories to see where the characters can be explored further. If there are any of the stories that you would like to read more about again, I'd love to hear from you!

Visit my blog at www.gacyharper.com

Join my newsletter for free exclusive previews
www.gacyharper.com/in

Follow me on Twitter at
http://www.twitter.com/gacyharper

Like my page on Facebook at
http://www.facebook.com/gacyharper

Discover my books at major ebook retailers everywhere.